CAT KILLER

CAT KILLER

Sandy Dengler

VICTOR BOOKS

A DIVISION OF SCRIPTURE PRESS PUBLICATIONS INC.
USA CANADA ENGLAND

95-217

Copyediting: Carole Streeter and Barbara Williams
Cover Design: Paul Higdon
Cover Illustration: John Dawson

Library of Congress Cataloging-in-Publication Data

Dengler, Sandy.
   Cat killer / by Sandy Dengler.
      p.   cm. —(Mirage mysteries; 1)
   ISBN 1-56476-137-1
   I. Title. II. Series: Dengler, Sandy. Mirage mysteries; 1.
PS3554.E524C37 1993
813'.54—dc20   93-1181
                                        CIP

1 2 3 4 5 6 7 8 9 10 Printing/Year 97 96 95 94 93

Contents

KING KONG CLIMBS

The frown on her face showed you what kind of a day she was having, and you could just bet the day had not yet finished heaping indignities and irritations upon her. With impatient resignation she unlocked the driver-side door of the baby-blue Geo she'd been riding in for twenty of the last forty-eight hours, and slid behind the wheel for one more short spin. She twisted the key in the ignition.

The hood lifted. The dash panel ripped apart. Its shrapnel flew past her and through her, followed almost instantly by the shock wave that crushed the front of her body. The windshield shattered upward as the windows burst out sideward. The roof began peeling back. The seat melted and then ignited. Two and a half seconds had elapsed since she turned the key, and she was already dead for one of them.

Joe Rodriguez admired professionalism — in a grudging way, even professional dirty work. And this was a professional job, start to finish.

The car had been baby blue once. Now it was black down to the rocker panels. Scorched, rumpled metal sulked where once it had shone smooth under a fresh wax job. Shattered glass and car shards lay wherever they had fallen, all over the motel parking lot. The backseat still smoldered. The frontseat was gone.

The driver, described by associates and one witness as a pretty black woman in her early thirties, was gone too. She was driver in name only, for turning on the ignition had touched it off. Professional job. The bomb left no doubt as to the cause of death and left precious little of the victim, but Maynard Rust's lab crew were swarming over the scene anyway. Their professionalism also piqued Joe's admiration.

Joe stood for a few minutes simply watching. The TV crews were all here, making the most of a visually spectacular event for the evening news, jockeying for camera angles, harassing the uniformed officers in hopes of getting just a little bit more. Pity that the videocams didn't capture the haunting stench.

Out by the curb, Gene Rivera kept gawkers moving. Even Gene looked efficient today. Now in the magical world of plainclothes middle ranks, Joe, like Gene, had started his police career on Phoenix street curbs orchestrating traffic. Joe had never really minded herding cattle. He knew Rivera detested it.

"Hey, Joe! Fella here to talk to you."

Joe walked across the lot to the yellow tape that kept at bay those gawkers beyond Gene's purview.

A young man, overgroomed and overdressed in a power-colored sport coat, paused beyond the line. "You're in charge here, right?"

Joe must have hesitated a tad too long, for the young man added, "Five feet eleven, 170 or so, dark hair and eyes, built sort of like Arnold Schwarzenegger, sport coat. You fit the description that blond gave me."

"She missed by a mile on the Schwarzenegger part, but I'll take what I can get. Sergeant Joe Rodriguez."

"Les Bowman. I'm the manager here. You seem to have just about the whole parking lot cordoned off. I was wondering if you might bring your ropes in a little closer. Leave more space for parking, you know?"

"We'll be done in a few hours, Mr. Bowman. We don't want to disturb any of that debris lying around, not until the lab people get done with it."

"Yes, but guests are coming in. We need all the . . . and the appearances, you know?"

"A few hours. We appreciate your cooperation very much. I'll be sure to mention it in the preliminary report."

"Hey! Look who's here!" Here came Gretchen Wiemer, the lab's official picture-taker. She performed other chores for Maynard besides photography and feats of forensic chemistry, and Joe knew by rumor what some of them were. Les Bowman muttered something indistinct as Joe moved off.

Her blond hair bobbed, bouncy as a shampoo commercial. It was unfortunate, in a way, that she was so tall. With her sexy spike heels, she nearly matched Joe's five-eleven. "I'm glad Jerry gave you this one." She grinned wickedly. "We need the comic relief." Her face sobered. She handed him a dozen thick photos. "Brought to you through the miracle of modern photographic processes: instant pictures of the destruction."

He leafed through them. "Why am I looking at instant photos when I have the whole gory display itself spread out before me?" She was an excellent crime photographer—had all the relevant stuff at just the right angles.

"Know what's wrong with you, Rodriguez? You're never impressed. I bet if King Kong climbed up that motel sign you wouldn't even notice."

"Sure I'd notice. He'd howl when he cut his toe on that broken Triple-A sign up there, and then I'd notice."

Her head whipped around and up; the hair followed belatedly. "I didn't see that. Doubt Maynard did, either. Think the bomb sent something up there to take it out?"

"Could be. Go find the manager, Les Bowman—you know, the powerfully dressed guy you described me to—and ask him if it was already broken. If not, snap one with your miracle of modern photographic processes there, before Maynard sends someone up."

"Will do." She swung a long leg over the rope and disappeared beyond onlookers.

He lingered a few moments more, but he wasn't

needed here. Maynard's crew cruised about, fully in their element, taking notes and photos and lab samples Joe would never dream of seeking. Professionalism. Joe walked over to the motel room.

Half a dozen techs and lab people wandered in and out, some in jumpsuits and some not. A cute little number with a pixie haircut—what was her name? Joyce?—even held the door for him. He smiled and said hello, but didn't greet her by name, just in case she wasn't Joyce.

The temperature was only about 80 outside—not at all that hot for Phoenix in April—but someone had cranked the air conditioner in this motel room up to the iceberg end of the dial. Persis Magen came from Waukesha, Wisconsin. No doubt for her, 80 degrees constituted an epic heat wave. Joe closed the door behind him and paused while his eyes adjusted to the dark and his skin adjusted to the cold.

His copper hair tousled as always, the insufferably Irish Tom Flaherty bounded up from the chair by the kitchenette. His lanky six-one frame and windmill elbows flailed at cross purposes with each other. "Joe, let me introduce ye around. The young lady with the charming freckles, seated on the edge of the bed there—Marie Kabrhan. And I'm pleased to present Mrs. Persis Magen here. Mrs. Magen, Marie, this be Joe Rodriguez, me brilliant partner, the lad who does all the thinking for us both."

Marie didn't stand, but she extended her hand. "Mr. Rodriguez, how do you do." Joe gave her his usual double handshake, taking her hand in his right and closing the left over them both to squeeze.

Hardly ever did anyone notice that his right hand had no grip. Marie didn't seem to, either.

With plain brown hair and large brown eyes, she wasn't exactly pretty. Or perhaps she was. Borderline. She had worked closely with the murder victim and knew her well. It showed in her drawn face. When she was feeling more herself, she probably looked very attractive.

Joe crossed to shake with Persis Magen. Again he used his make-do handshake, and Persis Magen noticed. Her eyes asked a question but her voice said nothing aloud. Alert and observant, this evangelist.

The lady looked much livelier, much younger than her pictures suggested. Photos didn't do her justice at all. Her gray hair swirled back into a soft bun. She couldn't be called overweight, but neither was she slim. Her hazel eyes locked onto yours and penetrated. Persis Magen, evangelist. By the measures of money generated and crowds drawn, she was as successful as any in the field.

Joe felt distinctly uncomfortable among these religion enthusiasts. Why did Jerry put him on this one, anyway? Except Joe knew that Jerry too got instantly antsy around anything religious. Give Joe the sticky ones, the unappealing ones—that was his lieutenant's standard operating procedure.

"Mr. Flaherty's been speaking highly of you, Mr. Rodriguez. I'm delighted." Her voice was obviously trained for radio.

"My honor, Mrs. Magen. And don't believe anything the Irishman says. Not only did he kiss the Blarney stone; he also drank heavily from the Hassayampa."

"The what?" Marie's voice was soft, musical, innocent. Joe liked her voice.

"'Tis an old Arizona legend, lass." Tom was deliberately thickening his brogue and Joe happened to know he saved the good stuff for ladies he wanted to impress. "First ye drink from the Hassayampa River. If then ye turns your face upstream, never again will ye speak a lie. But if 'tis downstream ye be turning, you'll never again speak the truth. And I cannot for the life of me remember which way I turned."

Marie smiled and Persis chuckled. Tom's gift for turning a morbid occasion into a bearable one doubtless came from the Irish skill of breathing joy into wakes. Joe perched on the foot of the queen-size bed as far from Marie as diplomacy permitted, and listened.

"Now. As we were discussing," Tom purred. "Marie, ye were sitting there mending a dress?"

"The seam had parted under the arm of her dress. Persis' dress. It happens a lot when she swings her arms around speaking. I was fixing it. Persis wanted to wear it to the gathering."

"Gathering?" Joe asked.

Persis chimed in. "When I arrive in town for a series of evangelistic meetings, it's not the beginning of the campaign but very nearly the end of it. A year ahead of time, we begin assembling groups of workers from the churches. They go door to door, meet regularly for prayer and study, prepare themselves to counsel new believers. Just before the meetings themselves begin, we all gather together for corporate prayer. The gathering."

"And since the first meeting's tonight, this prayer thing is this afternoon?" Joe glanced at his watch.

"Five P.M. Oh, dear. That's less than two hours. Would you mind asking questions faster? It's crucial that I attend."

"Of course." Tom rolled right along. "Mrs. Magen, ye were catching a wee bite to eat here at the counter. And Miss DuBois went out to fuel the car. Did ye send her or did she volunteer?"

"I don't remember. Do you remember, Marie?"

The girl shrugged. "I usually tend to that stuff. Cat's more Persis' personal secretary than gopher. But I was busy with the dress."

Two more of Maynard's techs wandered in and busied themselves in the kitchenette.

Joe frowned. "Cat? Gopher?"

"Catherine DuBois was Cat to us. A gopher—you know, a person who goes for things. I go-fer takeout food, go-fer the mail, go-fer the dry cleaning."

Joe knew that; why hadn't he thought of it? "And Miss DuBois—Cat—did secretarial chores primarily?"

Persis nodded. "She was a whiz at keeping a complicated calendar straight. I never once missed a meeting or an appearance. That was her function on the road. Personal correspondence. Phone. At home she arranged the calendar in advance of a trip, so as to make maximum use of our time. Gifted, that girl."

"Screening? That is, filtering the calls and callers you receive?" Joe noticed the telephone had been disconnected.

"Yes. People would be demanding twenty-four

hours of my day if it weren't for Cat."

"Billing and accounting?"

"No. Jules keeps an eye on that on the road. We hire an accounting firm, of course. Far too complex for one person. The offerings generated during the evangelistic meetings are handled by the local committee chairmen. We give the local churches a portion. The only finances we're directly involved with on the road are our personal and travel expenses."

"Ye haven't met Jules Robinson, Joe," said Tom, "nor have I. Mrs. Magen. Your reputation suggests you'd have a far larger entourage than ye actually do. Why travel so light? Or be there a motel full of ancillary folk elsewhere?"

She chuckled again, throaty and relaxed. "Ancillary folk . . . I like that. Our campaigns are almost completely home grown. The choir director's chosen from a local church. We hired ASU students to handle the stadium lighting and security. It's cheaper on the road to hire people who are familiar with the facilities than to bring in our own personnel. Particularly when so many donate their time as a Christian service."

Joe made mental notes about penny-pinching. Also, he wondered if the IRS were interested in this lady. And might they tap into her secretary for information? If they did, might this lady have found out about it and . . . He pulled his notebook and started jotting ideas.

For a woman who had just lost her close associate, Mrs. Magen seemed remarkably unmoved. Her hands lay quietly in her lap, her facial muscles moved naturally with her expressions. No tenseness, no sign of sorrow save for red, puffy eyes.

"Ye still haven't answered the original question, ladies. Did she volunteer or was she sent? Marie?"

The girl scrunched forward with her chin in her hands, her elbows on her knees. She scowled not at Tom but past him. Finally she shook her head. "I'm sorry. I can't remember the words at all. We work together pretty well as a team. When something needs doing, whoever's free at the moment does it. I can't remember who said what to whom. The tank was low; it was one more little thing that had to be done; Cat went out to do it."

"Did she say anything unusual? Do anything unusual?"

"No." Marie's face pinched together in concentration.

"Not just today. Recently. Anything at all extraordinary?"

"No. Just like always on the road."

"Mrs. Magen?"

"Nothing unusual. Cat was a steady woman. Quiet, kept to herself. Dependable. She didn't discuss thoughts or fears. Or joys, for that matter. I mention that to point out that just because we didn't notice anything out of the ordinary doesn't mean that there was nothing out of the ordinary. She was very good at keeping things to herself."

"Have ye any reason at all to suspect something unusual might have been happening in her life? Hints or feelings?"

Both women pondered, frowning. Both shook their heads.

Tom took off on a fresh tack. "Let's suppose for

the moment that the bomb be meant for someone else; perhaps Marie here, if she usually fills the tank. Perhaps for Mrs. Magen, assuming the killer didn't realize the tank was low. You, Mrs. Magen, get in to drive away to your gathering. Kaboom. Can either of ye think of any reason—any at all— that me supposition might have some validity?"

Joe watched the women play with that one awhile. Obviously they had already considered it, both of them.

Marie intrigued him. She was either very, very tired or very, very shrewd. The evangelist couldn't be called cheerful, but she remained upbeat, even glib. Did she have no affection at all for the murdered woman? And with the possibility that another victim was intended, could it be the bomb had been wired in the wrong car altogether? Joe jotted himself a note to check the motel registry for similar cars or any bearing New Mexico plates.

His thoughts changed lanes as Tom's technique grabbed his attention. Tom was a professional of the talking sort. In fact, other investigators in the department often brought tough interviews to him just to watch him work. He might crash right into an issue like a bowling ball into the pins. Or he might skate all around his subject, nipping at the fringe of it and darting off to other things.

Now he was toying with the prospect that Cat DuBois had not been the intended victim. To the casual ear he asked irrelevant questions by the dozen. Joe could see the thread, sometimes even anticipate a question, because he knew how Tom worked. The Irishman was weaving an elaborate net of data, bits and particles of information to reveal the inter-personal relationships of this evangelistic team 1,000 miles from home.

Joe's ears perked. "What'd you say, Miss Kab-rhan?"

"The notes. The threatening notes."

Tom stared at Persis.

The lady shrugged. "I get all manner of extremely emotional letters—everything from effusive thanks to dire threats. These were at the threat end of the spectrum."

"Ye didn't mention them before."

"I frankly never thought of them. Nearly every day the mail brings in a few letters from people who feel a woman has no business being an evangelist."

"More than one. When did the first arrive?"

Persis scowled. "What would you say, Marie? A month ago?"

"If it's the same person. They weren't signed."

Tom leaned both elbows on the kitchenette counter. "What did it say exactly?"

"I don't know." Persis shifted and glanced at her watch as she spoke. "I dismissed it as another crank—I get a lot of those too—and discarded it. 'Not deserving to live,' something like that."

"And then?"

"I really don't remember. The second was on the road somewhere. Similar sentiments. And the third—there were three, I believe—within the last day or two."

Joe broke in. "Mrs. Magen, you want to get to your gathering early, don't you?"

"Yes, I do."

"Tom, how about you take her in a black and white? We can talk again afterward. I saw Harry wandering around out front."

Persis bounced to her feet. "Gentlemen, I appreciate this immensely. A direct answer to prayer, leaving early."

Within moments Tom and Mrs. Magen were out the door. With the two most ebullient persons gone, the room felt suddenly empty, despite the two techs finishing up in the kitchenette.

Miss Kabrhan rubbed her face. That was another reason she looked plain. No makeup. She straightened. "I wonder."

She walked over to the formica slab that served as a desk and fished out a wastebasket. She settled in the middle of the floor and dumped the basket out in front of her.

Why not? He had nailed down the search warrant already, and something like this would definitely be included in his very general description. He always did that first. Now all he had to do was search. Meticulously, Joe folded up his legs and hunkered down opposite her. They sifted through the trash in silence, unrumpling papers and refilling the basket piece by piece.

Marie looked up briefly with baleful puppy-dog eyes. "When the maid came by, Persis was working on a message and didn't want to be disturbed. Cat spent the time polishing off the last two days' correspondence: answer, file, or toss."

"This is two days' worth?" Joe didn't get this much first-class mail in a year, except bills.

"Well, none of the mail that goes to Waukesha, of course. Just the stuff we got here in Phoenix. Not that many people write to her on the road; that's why there isn't very much."

Joe knew Tom would be asking questions all the way to the gathering. He and Harry would also act as bodyguards because quite possibly the evangelist needed some. She probably wouldn't realize that part of it. Joe should be covering the same ground Tom did, so that later they could compare the answers received. He lacked the gift for painless interrogation. Paper crackled in the silence.

"Here it is." Marie smoothed out a plain white paper and handed it to him. She continued fishing. "The envelope should be here somewhere. If I can remember . . . "

The note, on 6 by 9 plain linen paper, was no one's computer product, not even a fancy modern typewriter. It had been typed on a conventional machine with elite type, and excoriated the evangelist in a long rambling paragraph that hinted at lethal danger. It did not actually promise harm. Joe would study it in detail later.

He saw one machine in the room, over on the circular coffee table. Daisy wheel. "That your only typewriter?"

"Except for Cat's personal machine. Old as Methuselah and twice as hairy, but she never went anywhere without it."

"Where's that one?"

"Adjoining room. We book three linking rooms with kitchenette. Jules' and Henry's are separate, of course."

"Henry? Henry who?"

"Barbie. Jules is our advance man, confirming arrangements ahead of us. Henry's mop-up. He stays behind, makes sure all the bills are paid."

"I thought Jules took care of that."

She licked her lips and her voice faltered, as if she feared revealing some closeted skeleton. "Jules is not always the best organizer. And, uh, he's sometimes a bit slipshod about making certain everyone is taken care of. He, uh, tends to lack strong interest in people. Henry has unique spiritual gifts and he's very conscientious about making sure everyone is satisfied. He's brilliant at organizing discipleship groups and Bible studies. And he's very gentle. Nonthreatening. He's the best person to make sure all the loose ends are tucked in. Then he catches up to us."

"So he's still in Albuquerque?"

"That's right. Oh, hey. He has a typewriter too."

"Conventional elite?"

"Dancing ball, I think. But I don't remember. I'm sorry." She unfolded her legs and led the way to the connecting door. Her legs were remarkably long for her height—no more than five-five.

It took them a minute to find Cat's typewriter—she had slipped it into a large lower drawer. Joe fumbled the case latch. Now the carriage wouldn't move. Marie stepped in beside him and with a practiced flick hit a tiny lever. The carriage shivered, free at last.

She moved aside. "It locks in place when you're traveling. So you don't damage something knocking it around, I guess."

"I thought Cat was the only one who used it."

"I did for a week once, when the daisy wheel was down."

Joe snapped his pocketknife open and lifted one of the type arms with its tip. He pressed the letter against his finger and looked at the dent. Elite type. He locked the carriage back down. "I'll have to take this with me."

"You think that's the typewriter that—Cat? Can't be."

Joe shrugged, keeping it casual. "About half the typewriters in the world built like this one carry elite typeface. The others are pica. So if I gather up 50 percent of the nation's old style typewriters and dump 'em in Maynard's crime lab, he should eventually find the right one."

"I see. Routine?"

"Strictly. Let me write you a receipt before I forget." He patted his pockets. "Got a sheet of paper?"

Marie yanked drawers open one by one. No paper. No 6 by 9 linen pad, either. Joe stuck close enough to her to make sure.

"Never mind. I'll find one." Joe walked to the connecting door. "You mentioned looking for that envelope."

"Oh, that's right. I forgot." She went back out and dropped down beside her trash. Joe checked drawers here in Persis' room. Motel stationery. No 6 by 9 pad. He wrote Marie a receipt on a motel letterhead decorated with a two-color picture of the big free-standing motel sign, Triple A sign intact.

While Marie finished sifting through the trash for the white envelope, Joe took a second sheet of motel stock. He drew a crude picture of King Kong climbing up the sign, the ape's big toe covering the three A's.

He slipped it into Cat's typewriter case, for Gretchen.

HOT TIME IN THE OLD TOWN

Marie stood by the temporary bleachers at the ten-yard line, watching Persis Magen up on the dais between the goalposts. She looked around at the comforting faces of concerned men. Joe Rodriguez, three feet away from her, stood closest. Now there was a good-looking man—not pretty beauty, but a strong and gentle face with even features, black hair with a slight wave to it, a supple, medium build that he obviously kept in excellent shape.

Tom, the six-foot-one Irish detective with the non-stop patter, hovered close to the dais as if spring-loaded. He seemed to be a man in motion even when he was standing still. That kind of lean bundle of kinetic energy never ever gained an extra pound. The man would be just as skinny at age ninety as he was now.

She knew that other plainclothes officers peppered the crowd here and there, but she recognized only one, a tall, lanky man named Harry. They all blended in quite professionally.

Persis had, over Joe and Tom's objection, insisted the meetings not be postponed. Apparently Joe and these others had never attended a meeting such as this, nor understood the importance of it, but Marie had been through them a hundred times. Every time thrilled her anew, and this last part she loved best. In traditional circles it was termed "the altar call." Persis had completed her message about the ultimate work of Christ, but she didn't launch into the altar call immediately. She paused, biting her lip. It was the only external indication Marie ever saw that her employer was feeling nervous or upset.

Persis cleared her throat and began in a low voice. "Tonight on the news, if you've not seen it already, you'll learn that Persis Magen's personal secretary was murdered, killed by a car bomb. It's true. It happened a few short hours ago. Why, you ask, is Persis Magen feeling so fine when she has just lost one of her dearest friends? The answer is that Persis Magen knows exactly where Cat Dubois is this very moment.

"By the standards of the world Cat died untimely, in her prime. By God's timetable she is exactly where she ought to be right now, beholding the face of our risen Lord. I grieve. I will miss Cat until the day I also die. But I know with complete confidence"—the voice rose in triumph—"I'm totally assured that she's safe in eternal glory.

"You, my friends, can enjoy that same assurance.

I invite you to be ready for eternity from this moment on, by permitting Jesus to be the master of your life and your heart, and the guardian of your soul!"

She lifted her hands high in her characteristic gesture that rips out underarm seams. "Come! I invite you! Come to Jesus. Declare yourself for Him. Come with confidence and live from this moment on in confidence."

They came filing down the cement aisles by ones, by twos, by tens. Persis spoke encouragement at measured intervals.

Marie glanced at Joe. He half looked as if he wanted to join the growing crowd of new believers gathering before the dais. Had the message touched his heart, or did he simply suspect that trouble might lurk near?

This was the most beautiful moment of any night. Marie remembered her own tear-sodden conversion as Persis held not her hands, as counselors were doing here with new believers, but her head. Her sins had been washed away by the blood of Jesus; her cares and sorrows had been washed away by a river of tears.

Counselors from the local church met new believers one on one, greeted them, prayed with them, loved them. This was a key feature of Persis' evangelistic meetings, this careful discipleship. Every counselor had to be ready to make a full commitment to the nurturing and growth of the new believer entrusted to him or her. Normally more women than men came forward. Tonight the ratio seemed closer to fifty-fifty.

Here came the dangerous part. Persis stepped down off her dais into the churning crowd to speak to each new believer personally, to touch a shoulder, to shake a hand. Tom and Harry flanked her closely, watching everywhere. Joe moved closer not to Persis but to Marie. She watched his profile a few moments. He had absolutely no interest in what had just been said. His eyes darted. He stood tense, ready to bolt. He was working. Obviously, this was just another job to him.

The bleachers emptied but the mass on the field lingered. The full moon edged up over the far stadium roof. Tom and Harry seemed to be hustling Persis along, inching her toward the exit tunnel. Half a dozen pastors slowed her with questions and comments, a dozen others were gently rebuffed by two men Marie decided must also be officers. And now Persis, Marie and all were bathed in the blue-green light of the tunnel. Doors closed behind them. It was over.

Marie grasped both Persis' hands and kissed her on the cheek, "It's the best you've ever presented that theme, I think."

"Thank you, Marie. Praise His name. Gentlemen, I feel like the President of the United States with all these bodyguards. May I treat you to late dinner somewhere?"

"Very nice of you, ma'am, but we gotta be getting home." Harry mumbled something to Joe and led the way out into the warm night air.

They waited in silence by the huge doors as Tom brought the car around. Marie never ceased to marvel at the way those big parking lot lights changed pretty colors into ghastly shades. If this was the same car they arrived in, it was a lovely blue. In this light it looked like death in a thundermug.

Joe held the front passenger door for Marie, then crawled in back beside Persis. He looked very tired. "Home, James."

Tom grinned as the car bolted forward. "That's Seamus, not James. Erse, ye know."

"Shamus?" asked Marie. "Oh. Detective, you mean?"

"Me middle name.' Tis the Gaelic form of James, so the Chicano bloke was half right."

"Chicano bloke." Marie giggled.

"Mixed parentage." Tom seemed in rare form, waving one hand or the other, tucking in and out among cars. "His grandfather was full-blooded Yaqui Indian, his grandmother Mexican, and his mum's side is English. Across-the-big-water English. Did I get that right, Joe?"

"Jose Maria Jesus Rodriguez y Smythe. You got it all, Tom."

"And meself? Galway Irish, both sides. Now tell us of yourself, fair lass. Kabrhan sounds like some Mideast philosopher."

"Slovak."

"Slavic?"

"Slovak. Czechoslovakian. My great-grandparents came from Zvolen in Stredoslovensky. The family dropped the H for a few generations, trying to look American. I decided I was proud of the H, so I put it back where it belongs."

"Ah! A romantic ye are! Marvelous! The world needs more romance." Tom flipped a right so quickly Marie tipped forward.

Cat. Tom and Persis were talking about Persis' name, which led to the Persis of Romans 16, but Marie didn't listen. She had worked elbow to elbow with Cat for over two years. Suddenly, Cat was gone. The whole day ripped her nerves, so unreal. Cat would be waiting for them at the motel. Once in a great while, when work piled up, she missed the meetings themselves. Surely she'd pop up at the motel. She'd come in with Jules tomorrow. She wasn't completely gone.

Marie gasped and jerked, awakened by a gentle hand on her shoulder. Joe's. It was time to get out of the car. She felt mildly embarrassed to have fallen asleep amid such charming company and she said so. But mostly she felt groggy, overly tired. She stumbled zombielike into the motel room. A man in a sport coat materialized, talked to Joe a moment and then disappeared. They must have been keeping an eye on the room here.

Tom, all business, whipped out a pencil and notebook. "I'm taking orders. Anything in Phoenix is yours. Just name it. Chinese? Mexican? Fast food?"

Joe walked directly off into the adjoining room. His voice called, "How about a bucket of chicken?"

Tom's pencil poised above the paper. "Objections? Anyone overrule him? Agree with him?"

Persis kicked her shoes off and stretched out in the plastic chair. "Where do you plan to get chicken at this hour?"

"Phoenix, milady, has everything at any time, if ye just know where to look."

From the other room, Joe called, "Tommy is a

professional eater. Our coworkers call him the Stomach. He knows every single food source in the city: restaurant, deli, fast food, supermarket. You really do have a full range of choices, even at this hour."

Persis chuckled gently. "Chicken sounds fine. Get a box of mashed potatoes, please; or perhaps you people want french fries. I'd like a tall cola."

"Smashoes, fries, and cola. Joe? To drink?"

Joe paused to close the connecting doorway behind him. "Pick up a quart of milk."

"We have lots of milk here," Marie offered.

The pencil scritched. "Smashoes, fries and cola, hold the milk. Marie?"

"Cola. Lots of ice."

"All in and all done?" Tom glanced around. "I shall return forthwith." And he bounded out the door.

Persis wiggled her toes. "Where does that young man get so much energy at this time of night?"

Joe rattled a wastebasket in the bathroom. "He's like that constantly. Makes a whirling dervish look like siesta at Cuernavaca. I can't keep up with him." He appeared, stretched mightily, and draped himself across the counter that divided the kitchenette from the rest of the room. He looked as spent as Marie felt.

Persis lurched to her feet. "I'm taking a shower. I should be finished by the time our Irish dervish returns, and you gentlemen can resume your interrogation. The bathroom's harmless, I trust?"

"Appears so." Joe smiled.

Persis rummaged through the clothes on the pole,

found her robe and closed the bathroom door behind her. Silence.

Marie thought she had better move or she'd fall asleep again. She crossed to the kitchenette. "I'll get you a glass of milk now, if you like."

Joe stood erect. "Let me get it . You look ready to melt."

"I'm fine. Really." She glanced at him, feeling almost guilty for the lie. Their eyes locked and held. She would have smiled but she couldn't manage it. The tears boiled up and overflowed. He cared. She could tell by his eyes, lovely eyes dark and deep-set, that he cared.

Cat. She couldn't see anymore. His arms wrapped around her and held her tight while she let it all spill. A whole day of grief came out in five minutes of violent sobbing. Cat. Aloof, efficient Cat. Never a real friend, but for years a family member.

Did Persis hear her wild weeping? Surely so. But Persis always knew when to be there and when not to. Marie pulled herself back together by degrees, the conscious self almost detached from the abstract grieving self.

Joe pushed a handkerchief into her hand. She soaked it instantly. His voice was smiling. "Sorry I don't have any tissue. Hope your nose is tough." She heard a little *bdipp* and he stuck a paper towel in her hand.

He backed her up to a bar stool. She sat down on it and pulled a couple more paper towels off the open roll *bdipp bdipp*. Except for an occasional shuddering sob that kept surprising her, she had it pretty well in hand again.

"Sorry. I appreciate you, I really do. And here I thought cops were all sort of detached."

"I am detached. She wasn't my friend. May I get *you* a glass of milk?"

"Let me, please. I'll make it now." She slid off the stool and brought a glass tumbler down from the shelf. Her hands still shook. On second thought, she'd like some too. She reached for another glass. It slipped from her fingers and shattered on the floor. "What the matter with me?"

"I break glasses too, but I don't have any excuse. You do." He came around the end of the counter, dropped down and began picking up glass splinters. Nearly in tears again, Marie squatted to help.

The front window crashed. The ear-splitting boom, the blinding orange flash and the darkness all happened instantly. Joe's weight slammed against her in the blackness, mashed her against a cabinet. Her ears howled.

Moments later, his weight fell aside. With difficulty she wiggled out from under. Beyond the counter somewhere, faint and flickering orange light broke the darkness.

"Joe!" She reached out groping. She latched onto what was probably his arm and shook it. "Joe?"

He gulped a chunk of air with a single shuddering breath. He moved, then, and gulped air again. The arm jerked in the darkness as he pulled himself to sitting.

"Joe?"

"Stay down." Another gulping, wrenching breath. "Stay here." The arm yanked out from under her hand. He stood up, wavering, and braced for a moment against the counter. The orange flicker lighted his face dramatically as he tried to get his breath back. She could see a gun clasped in his two hands. He disappeared beyond the counter.

She couldn't just lie here. She clambered to her feet. With his jacket Joe was beating at little flames in the curtains and the carpet. The hideous orange glow winked out.

Persis! Until this moment Marie hadn't even thought of her. The bathroom door gaped open, shattered, the light still on in there. Joe hurried toward the light; so did Marie.

She paused in the doorway. Beyond the clear plastic shower curtain, a vague shadow sat scrunched in the corner of the stall. Joe whipped the curtain aside, dropped his smoky, dirty coat over the shadowed form and turned the water off.

Marie had to do something. "I'll call for help!" She wheeled away but Joe grabbed her arm.

"You stay right here. If you hear anyone out there—any unfriendly noise at all—scream bloody murder, understand?"

Marie nodded.

He darted away. She heard him rattle the phone. No phone, obviously. She couldn't remember if they had even hooked it back up this evening. She heard him running outside. Voices in the distance called and marveled and asked things.

Persis was climbing to her feet. Marie helped her up and steadied her as she stepped out of the shower stall. Marie closed the lid on the throne and Persis sat down, still clutching the grimy coat around her.

Persis took a deep breath, and when she spoke her voice was as firm as ever. "Oh, dear. I certainly hope he wasn't wearing his coat when all this happened to it."

"He put out a fire with it. I think someone owes him a new coat. Are you all right?"

"I suspect he'll have trouble collecting. Yes, I'm fine. The noise startled me and I slipped; that's all. Hand me my robe there, please, and help me dry off. I feel a bit shaky."

"Shaky! I should think so!"

"How did you two manage to escape unscathed?"

"We were down behind the counter. I dropped a glass and . . . " Marie stopped. "If I hadn't dropped that glass, we would've been right out . . . Joe would've. . . ."

"Try not to babble, dear. Thank our God for what He just did. Praise His name properly; you've been delivered. Make certain Detective Rodriguez learns the source of our salvation; I sense he's as yet unsaved. And help me with this robe."

Marie played lady-in-waiting to Persis, but her mind soared elsewhere. Salvation. Yes. Not just eternal salvation, but temporal salvation, easily seen and relished and appreciated. He was probably in the motel office calling in. No, he was surely on his way back by now. She remembered his crushing weight hurled against her. She recalled her own wild panic when he couldn't breathe.

What shocked her most was the realization of where her mind had been in those horrid moments. Much as she loved Persis, her only thoughts had been for Joe Rodriguez.

WISEACRES

Again all the parking slots that nosed against the motel walkway were either full or cordoned off. Joe parked in a truck slot in the middle of the asphalt. He straightened slowly, deliberately. He extricated himself from his MG as an eighty-year-old arthritic would unfold from a rocking chair. So this is what it feels like to be aged.

Maynard Rust's white van was backed up to the kitchenette with the smashed front window. Ten A.M. His people were probably about through by now. Joe walked over to the kitchenette four doors beyond.

Tall, lanky Harry Wallace always looked to Joe like a giraffe in a cop disguise. He grinned devilishly as he stepped aside out of the doorway. "Morning, Joe."

"Morning, Harry. Quiet, I presume. Tom here yet?"

"Not yet. Hey, I hear that your little Marie there is

one dynamite date."

"Y'know, Harry," Joe rapped on the door, "I smell a whole lousy day of one-liners coming on."

Persis' voice called from inside. Joe entered cautiously, lest he intrude upon some strictly feminine activity. Persis, still in her bathrobe, perched on the edge of an easy chair, if motel chairs can be called such. Papers and books lay spread out on the floor in a vast semicircle around her.

She looked up and smiled. "Good morning, Sergeant Rodriguez. This evening's message fried last night, so I must rewrite. You aren't disturbing anything. Help yourself to coffee, please."

Marie came out of the bathroom still drying her face. "Good morning, Joe. Coffee over there. Tom called about twenty minutes ago. He's with Jules who came in this morning, and asked me to tell you he'll be here shortly."

"Thank you." The coffee smelled good. These clever people brought their own coffee maker with them. He found mugs in the second cupboard he tried. Sugar? Here it was. Marie settled onto a stool across the counter.

The outside door burst open. Joe realized his hand was on his gun. Persis didn't notice. Marie did.

Gretchen Wiemer breezed in like a ray of blond sunshine. "Hi, Joe. You look like forty miles of bad road. Take two aspirin and call me in the morning."

Joe waved a hand around. "Persis Magen, may I present Gretchen Wiemer. She's with our crime lab. Gretchen, this is Marie Kabrhan."

"How'd ya' do. Delighted." Gretchen nodded

around and plopped down on a bar stool. "Here's
the prelims from last night and some notes from
this morning. Hack's bringing the supplementals
later. Interesting stuff. Hey, I need a cigarette."

Joe glanced at Persis.

Gretchen turned around to her. "Do you object if
I smoke?"

"No, dear." Persis was scrawling notes in the
margins of a legal pad.

Joe fished a new pack out of his inside pocket
and broke the cellophane. Out of the corner of his
eye he saw Marie looking at him, visibly disappointed. What difference should it be to her? Phooey on
her. He wouldn't even bother to explain. He shook
some loose, pointed the pack at Gretchen and dug
for his matches.

"Coffee?" Marie stretched for a mug.

"Sure. Thanks." Gretchen pulled a cigarette.
"You really do look terrible, Joe. But then that's
what you'd expect. You should know better than to
get bombed out of your mind at all hours of the
night."

"That's two."

"Who scored first? Harry? Miss Kabrhan, do you
recognize this?" From her bag of tricks, Gretchen
removed a ziptop evidence bag holding a piece of
charred leather and laid it on the counter. She blew
smoke and scowled at the cigarette in her hand.
"You gotta get Tom to change brands. Phew! These
are awful."

Marie's head snapped up. "Those are Tom's?"

Joe stirred his coffee. It was finally cooling off
enough to sip. "Tom picks the worst times to run

out of cigarettes. Like 3 A.M. Or in the middle of the desert. Or on stakeout behind some warehouse. I've saved us 1,000 hours of searching for all-night minimarts by carrying a spare pack for him." He hadn't meant to, but he ended up explaining anyway.

Marie picked up the evidence bag and studied the piece of leather from several angles. "It sounds silly, but I do believe I can identify this. At one time it was the side gore of Persis' flexible overnight bag."

Gretchen swung around on her stool and carried it to Persis. The lady studied it a moment. "Marie is right, I believe. An unstructured bag about so big by so big." She gestured with her hands. "The bag Jules accidentally left behind in Tulsa."

Joe sipped at his coffee and wished it would make him more alert. "Your mop-up man, what's his name? Henry Barbrie? Perhaps he found it."

Marie shook her head. "We called him that night. And also from Albuquerque. He wasn't able to turn it up."

Gretchen nodded. "Thank you both very much." She tucked it away again, gently, lovingly, as a saleslady would handle a porcelain figurine. "Oh, incidentally, Joe. King Kong's big toe came through. We found a nice little chunk of car up there. Maynard sends regards. Later."

"Later."

"Pleased to meet you both." Gretchen breezed out, taking her coffee with her. The door didn't close behind her; Tom was breezing in.

"Alloo, Gretch! And the top of the morning to ye all!" He nodded toward Persis. "Mrs. Magen."

Tom perched on the stool Gretchen had just vacated. Joe didn't bother to ask. He dug out a mug for Tom and poured. His ribs ached, especially in back.

"Marie, lass, you're looking fit as fine silk this morning. A far sight better'n this brute. Waiting for me long, Joe?"

"Overslept. I just got here. You linked up with Jules Robinson?"

"Aye. He's back at the office finishing a statement. Bruce will send him over then. These Maynard's prelims?" Tom scooped up the sheaf of paper and leafed through, grunting now and then. He picked up his coffee mug absentmindedly and burned his lips.

Persis stood up and stretched. "Sergeant Rodriguez, you're aware of the condition of our wardrobe. Every dress has one sleeve burned off. Marie and I must do some clothes shopping. The stores are all open now, don't you think?"

"Near 10. Surely so. Let Harry and Chen drive you around. They know where everything is." Joe knew, and doubtless these women knew, that Harry and Chen were bodyguards. Why dwell on it?

"'Scuse me, Mrs. Magen." Tom wiggled a finger. "You'll just be walking into Goldwater's in your bathrobe there?"

"Of course." Marie smiled. "If these Arizona girls can go shopping in swimsuits, we can shop in bathrobes. On the other hand, maybe we can sneak her in the back while I go out front and choose something off the rack for her. We'll work on it."

"There's a clever lass!"

"We'll try to be back in an hour or two." Marie smiled and nodded toward Joe and he returned in kind. She might be acting more cheerful today, but the lines in her face still betrayed her mourning. She had an interesting way of moving—very flexible, graceful, slightly exaggerated. She didn't exactly strut and flounce, but she executed every move crisply, with confidence. He really liked the way she moved.

As Tom saw them out the door into Harry's care, Joe settled himself carefully on the other stool. He was starting on his second cup when Tom returned to sprawl across stool and counter.

"No fooling, Joe. Want to go back to bed for another twenty-four hours? I'll cover. Ye really look bombed out."

"That's three. I'm all right. You're wagging your tail like a pup in a dog food factory. What's up?"

"Methinks we have a suspect. Tell me your impressions of Persis, her reactions to all this."

"I'd say she's weird, but Marie claims she's acting normally. No matter what happens she takes it in stride, bends with it, calls it God's will."

"God's will, aye."

"Marie started waxing hot on it last night so I let her go. Apparently yesterday was typical as an example. Persis prayed that she could get to her gathering in time. Presto. And it didn't faze her a bit that we ostensibly answered her prayer. Or God did. She actually expected it."

"And I got the same, in roundabout fashion, talking to Persis on the way to her gathering. She needs. She prays. She gets. No sweat. When were ye talking to Marie?"

"After the bomb and before you got back with the chicken. Marie seemed anxious for me to know we were all saved from death by direct divine intervention. Persis in the shower, Marie and I because of the glass she dropped. Marie's attitude, I think, is an adjunct of Persis'. If God's ready for you, you'll die regardless. And if He doesn't want you yet, no one on earth can get you."

" 'T'would simplify matters for the homicide squad, aye?"

Joe sat thinking about Marie's conversation last night. She expressed her religious views ardently, but you'd expect that from a member of a traveling evangelistic team. She pitched Persis' party line, no doubt, and you'd expect that also. Was he going to get constant sales pitches for God while working this case? And why was she picking on him and not Tommy? Heaven knows Tom needed it more than he did.

"You said a suspect?"

Tommy beamed. "In browsing through Maynard's thing of beauty here I find no contradictions. This Jules Robinson's a real pill. Tall and blond and skinny except for a big potato butt. A truly gross individual. Not as bad as Harry, but skinny. Pimples. Twenty-two going on five. What ye call backward socially."

"Retarded?"

"Not exactly. Flaky but not nuts. Seems smart enough. Ye needn't tell him twice. He just can't put two and two together worth diddly. Anyway, he let Cat out of the bag, literally. So I did some checking in records; he's right on all counts."

Joe shifted, trying to find a comfortable position for his back. There wasn't any. He started to draw a deep breath and cut that short in a hurry.

Tom extracted a wad from his inside pocket. He spread photos and his hastily-penned notes all over the counter. "This is Catherine DuBois, alias Cat. Alias Catherine French, alias French Katy. Busted any number of times for illegal possession, beat a manslaughter rap, arrested for dealing, no conviction. Hooker but no convictions for prostitution."

Joe studied the three photos. Two were standard mug shots, the third a group snapshot. Cat stood in the middle, her arm around Persis on one side and Marie on the other. All were smiling. Cat DuBois had been an exeedingly attractive and dignified-looking black woman with velvet coffee-with-cream skin. Even her pictures said "efficiency" and "aloofness." She wore the regal air of an African queen.

Tom rattled on in high gear. "She met Persis about three years ago and was converted. Put her sordid past behind her so completely that some of her closest workers didn't know about her. Marie, for instance."

"But Jules knew."

"Aye, Jules knew. He pointed me directly to specifics—where to look for information on Cat's past, clear back to her birthplace, Shreveport. He also claims that Cat had her hooks into Persis for a tidy sum monthly. He has access to the books, ye see."

"Hush money."

"The very thing. Jules believes Cat never got out

of the chemical industry, just got smarter. Used Persis' operation as a front for her own little sideline, though he hastens to remind me that's just conjecture on his part. Not firsthand."

"Persis would stand still for that?"

"Jules thinks Persis found out and decided to pay off instead of scream. I mean, how would it look if this marvelous evangelist could not point to her own secretary as a success story? If the truth about Cat be known, t'would cut into Persis' credibility and thereby into her pocketbook. Damage her business. Ye know how any little misstep can ruin an operation like this if the media latched onto it, and surely they would."

"Surely. So Cat gets destroyed instead." The coffee suddenly lay very heavy on Joe's stomach. He stirred in a second dollop of sugar. "Did this Jules actually come out and express the thought that Pesis is a murderer?"

"I doubt the prospect has occurred to him. He feels, I think, that it might just as well have been some compatriot in crime of Cat's, a slighted dealer or supplier. Or possibly, another person inside the organization, some nervous sort who's afraid of the damage such revelations would cause. Apparently we have scores of suspects hiding behind the agency facade in Waukesha." Tom tapped the pile of paper. "Maynard's notes here say the bomb arrived in a leather bag; plastiques not too easy to get; professional setup; couple other details."

"Gretch has this but it's not in the supplementals yet. The bag belonged to Persis, supposedly left behind in Tulsa by Jules. He drives the company car?"

"Aye."

"The company only has one car?"

"On the road, aye. Not economical to take two, he claims."

"The car yesterday was a rental. Why does Persis rent her wheels and leave the company vehicle to her subordinate? Why doesn't she take dibs on her own wheels and have Jules toodle around in a rental? Why don't they fly?"

"Crossed me mind, so I asked. First, the company car always goes on tour with them except overseas. They want accessible wheels on the ground should any little thing go wrong with the flight schedule. Jules, making himself to be a ninja turtle or some other pop cultural hero, boasts he's saved their blessed fannies more'n once that way. Second, Jules takes a paternal interest in the car. Feels it's at his disposal. Now here I'm reading twixt the lines, but as I listen to this Jules, methinks Persis lets him have his way rather than put up with his tantrums."

"She'd pay car rentals to avoid a scene with her employee? She seems too authoritarian for that."

"She doesn't pay. There's a Christian rental agent in Albuquerque who gave her access to the car as long as she should need it. She's to leave it in Riverside when she recommences her airborne itinerary."

"Unfortunately, it becomes an insurance write-off. What do you have on Jules?"

"No time yet. That's next. Joe, kidding aside, what ye should be doing is going over to emergency. Let Asimoto check ye out. I know better'n to think ye will, but at least lie down awhile. You're turning green. Much as an Irishman loves green, I hate to see ye thus."

"These people seem so wholesome, Tommy."

"We haven't proven anything."

"Right. We just see a lot of dirty fingers pointing." Joe pushed his coffee mug away and rubbed his eyes. They burned. "Why can't people who are supposed to be clean and upstanding ever be clean and upstanding, without all these dirty little secrets in their closets? All right, let's say Cat was mucking around like Jules thinks. So she fried. She asked for it. Let's say we pin it on Persis or one of her subordinates. Who loses? Who's the big loser who didn't ask for any of this?"

"The sweet little heroine in this mellerdrammer. Sure, when fate isn't twisting Marie into hard knots, she be cute as a kitten."

"Too cute to hurt."

"Now you're getting sentimental, me chum, and that's fatal in this line of work. Come along." Tom grabbed Joe's arm and pulled sideways. Joe stuck his foot out barely in time to catch his balance. Tom stiff-armed him firmly, piloted him to the nearest bed and toppled him with a gentle shove. "Lie there. Don't move. Sleep. When the ladies get back we'll work on them independently. We draw straws to see who gets Marie. Meself has first choice, best two out of three if I lose. Night, night."

Tom turned his attention to raiding the refrigerator and Joe turned his to this religion business. Marie. One of the nicest things about her was this aura of purity and faith. Then there was Persis, but after Koresh and Jim Jones and his Jonestown, who can trust an evangelist?

Was Persis the pure servant of God the outside world saw? Or was she a murderer who purchased the death of the convert who had betrayed her? Did she then hide in the shower to escape the second bomb ordered to cover her guilt by making herself appear the target? Even if she were not the murderer, how far would she go as a Christian leader in glossing over Cat's alleged illicit activities? Joe really wanted to ponder these questions more thoroughly, but he fell asleep.

A Policeman's Lot

Joe resisted the impulse to wave bye-bye as Ron Turcatto slipped into the backseat of a charcoal gray Mercedes. In the front seat sat Persis, already deep in conversation with the driver, an intense, mustachioed young man in a suit altogether too stuffy and dark for Phoenix in April. Beside Turk, lucky Turk, slight little Marie Kabrhan settled into the lush upholstery. The Mercedes pulled away from the motel door and waddled cautiously out into traffic.

Harry Wallace folded up like a carpenter's rule and inserted himself into an unmarked department car. He and Chen drove out of the lot and fell in behind the Mercedes. Persis was on her way to a prayer luncheon of some sort and Joe and Tom faced desk work the afternoon. Probably *all* afternoon.

At Joe's elbow, Tommy giggled. "Methinks yon

Harry Wallace coasted through the police academy on a basketball scholarship."

"Naw. Worked his way through washing windows. He's the only person on the metro payroll who can clean the transom windows in the old courthouse without using a ladder. Ever play pickup basketball with him?"

"No. He good?"

Joe grimaced. "Seventy-three elbows, and two or three of 'em always flying at you. The guy's got the coordination of a drunk spaz; you can't gauge where any of his body parts will be from moment to moment. He's a menace to his teammates."

"Then 'tis a fine thing the academy has no basketball team."

"It's saved a lot of lives. What's this?" Joe nodded toward an approaching woman.

A diminutive older lady came marching toward them with grim determination. She would have had to wear elevator shoes to match a ten-year-old in stature, but there was a delicate power about her that suggested she swam laps every day. Her short, silvery hair gleamed in the sun as she planted herself in front of Joe. She democratically included Tom in her scowl as well. "Are you two the policemen harassing Mrs. Magen?"

How should he answer this? Joe always had trouble with do-you-still-beat-your-wife questions. "Can we help you?"

"You're Mexican."

"Partly."

She turned to Tom. "You look Irish. You're of Irish extraction?"

He laid his accent on thick. "No extraction, madam. The real McCoy, so to speak."

"Roman Catholic! Foreigners! Irish and Mexican foreigners. Of course. That explains your persecution of Mrs. Magen. The papist hatred of the true church."

Joe wagged his head. "Sorry, ma'am. This is all going by me. If you'd like to file a complaint..." He pulled a card from his jacket pocket. "Here's our lieutenant. He handles complaints."

She took the card but it didn't soften her glare. "You're opposing God, you know. You'll pay for it in eternity, mark my words. You and all those who offend God will pay. Persis Magen is His servant, ordained by—"

Tom interrupted her, and he hardly ever interrupted anyone. "Did ye see those two fine gentlemen who left in the car behind Mrs. Magen? One was quite tall, the other of Oriental persuasion. Nor be they foreigners. Now those two be the very ones to whom ye ought speak. They're directly involved, ye see, and we're but peripheral to the whole case. We wouldn't want your valuable advice to fall upon ears other than those best prepared to receive it. They understand the situation. We do not ken your meaning."

Joe glanced at his watch. "Time for those phone calls. They're waiting."

"Aye. We'd best get cracking." Tom extended his hand. "We appreciate your interest in us, Mrs.— ah . . . Mrs.?"

She did not shake. "*Miss* Arburton. You're trying to dump me and you're being disgustingly obvious about it. You'd better listen. You're taking me much too lightly, both of you. You're just as guilty. You don't . . . "

"Duty calls. Me pleasure, Miss Arburton!" Tom ducked toward the parking lot. "Come, Jose."

"Ma'am." Joe nodded toward the wizened lady and jogged off after Tom.

Little knots of people still hung around here and there, even though workmen had nearly completed repair of the bomb damage. Vultures. Hundreds of people in this city were dying slowly, ingloriously, of AIDS or cancer or whatever, and these gawkers couldn't care less. But let someone die spectacularly, with lots of bells and whistles. . . .

Joe slid behind the wheel of his Midget as Tom twisted enough to get his lanky legs stuffed in under the dash. "What do you make of that?" Joe asked. He torched off the engine and gunned it a little.

"Meself has a theory I call the Flaherty Theory of Pubs. Ye walk into any pub—here, Ireland, anywhere. The clientele ye meet therein be only those few who frequent pubs, and not the backbone of the country, who all be home with their family and friends. A small, small segment."

"I doubt Miss Arburton is a frequenter of pubs." Joe pulled out into the street and headed west.

"True. But expand me thesis. Methinks, applying this theory to the matter at hand, that our Miss Arburton be a small, small segment who takes religion just a wee bit too seriously, and not one of those forming the backbone of the faith."

"Who are all at home with their family and friends."

"Or in church or engaged in charitable ventures or whatever. Ye ken me point?"

"I ken. This doesn't have anything to do with your Flaherty Theory of Poof, right?"

"Nor me Flaherty Theory of Plastic."

"Plastic?"

Joe spent both lunch and the drive downtown learning about the world's love of destroying or refusing the real thing, and then replacing it with artificial replicas carefully designed to look just like the real thing. Tommy expounded at length on gas fireplace logs instead of firewood, of plastic philodendron and silk flowers. He had a point.

They entered police headquarters by the side hall because a TV truck was parked out front. TV reporters are persons diligently to be avoided. They took the back stairs up.

"You!" Grace Red Morning, her short black hair slightly askew and her strong, smooth Navajo features definitely ruffled, rose from her reception/switchboard station. She faced Joe, and she was pointing her finger—nay, her whole arm. "You!"

"Now what'd I do? Good afternoon, Grace."

"I must hie meself yon!" Grinning, Tommy ducked in the door, but Joe was neither fast enough nor lucky enough.

Grace roared, "Look at my switchboard!"

"There are lights on it."

"Constantly! And people down in the lobby waiting for you. Now I don't mind fielding calls if you put out a legitimate request for information, but this is absurd. Maddening. Don't you ever do this to me again."

"I don't understand."

"Don't play dumb with me. I swear I'm gonna get you for this, Joe Rodriguez!" She sat down with a plop and flicked a switch. Her voice shifted from enraged to pleasant, instantly. "Homicide. How may I help you?" Professionalism. Joe admired it.

He entered the squad room door and walked three feet toward his desk when Janet James, seated at her own desk, stuck her arm out. She handed him half a dozen while-you-were-out slips. "Calls for you, you jerk."

"Peace and joy to you too. Thanks." He sifted idly through the slips—no one he knew—as he walked, and stopped cold. A pile of yellow slips just like these lay on his desk. Dozens of them. Maybe hundreds.

Mel Carter, sandy blond and boyishly handsome, claimed the desk next to Joe's. He stood up and stretched far enough to toss still more of the slips onto Joe's desk. "Glad you're back. I'm sick of answering your phone."

"Whatever happened to voice messaging? And what is all this, anyway?" Joe glanced at Tommy's desk across from his. Nothing. "And how did you escape?"

Tommy shrugged, with a what-can-I-do? grin. "'Twas not me name in the papers, nor me name on the Hour of Glory show this morning. Chen mentioned it. Chuckling, he was."

"Hour of Glory? What?" Joe plopped into his chair. His phone rang. His mind still at sea, he picked it up. "Rodriguez."

"My name is Lucille Crane, Mr. Rodriguez. I'm

calling to protest the persecution of Persis Magen."

"What?" This was not happening. Totally surreal. Joe listened politely without listening at all. Lucille Crane, whoever Lucille Crane was, babbled on about the legions of evil. Joe stirred through the yellow slips.

"Whoa!" It came barking out of him so sharply the voice on the line fell silent. "Miss Crane. Mrs. Crane."

"It's Mrs."

"Mrs. Crane. Do you want to truly help out, or are you just calling to hear yourself talk?"

"What? What do you mean?"

"Will you help me?"

"Not in your mindless persecution, no. Of course not."

"Help *me*. Personally." Joe sat back in his chair and tried to keep his words marching in a straight line to his point. "Mrs. Crane, I just arrived back from lunch and here on my desk are over 100 yellow slips of paper. Phone calls made to me in the last few hours. All are from persons I've never met. None has a call-back number. They all say essentially the same thing. Protest, protest, protest. I've no idea exactly what anyone is protesting, and until I do, I've no idea how to improve matters. Will you please—can you, please—enlighten me as to what's going on here? What prompted your call? What prompted all these others?"

"I feel safe in assuming you didn't listen to Hour of Glory this morning."

"You may safely assume I've never heard of Hour of Glory. What is it?"

"Why am I not surprised? Radio, AM 801. Brother Larry Jennings from Glory Desert Assembly. Each morning he conducts a brief worship and praise service. But before that he reports news of Christian importance. He gives God's perspective on world and local events. It's excellent. Much better than the atheistic liberal bias of the regular news programs."

Joe thought, *Bias? You call the regular news biased?* But keen diplomat that he was, he kept it to himself. "And he reported on the fatal car bomb and incident at the motel. But that was yesterday."

"That's right. Today he followed the news segment with his own editorial comment regarding what happened."

"Ah. Now we're getting somewhere. In that commentary he urged his listeners to make their opinion known, is that correct?"

"Yes." Her voice sounded less strident, less supercilious.

"I appreciate that you're taking the time to help out here, Mrs. Crane, I really do. Can you explain his editorial opinion? Briefly and succinctly, please."

"Well, I don't know how succinctly..." The voice paused. "Mr. Rodriguez, you know there are very few people these days who would use a word like 'succinctly,' let alone use it properly. It's a pleasure talking to someone who respects the language."

"My mother taught English. She made it a cardinal sin in our house to dangle a participle. What is Mr. Jennings' editorial opinion?"

Silence for a moment, apparently as the woman

arranged her thoughts. "The spirit of evil—that is, Satan—is diametrically opposed to the spirit of good, which is the trinitarian God. When one waxes, the other waxes. When one wanes, the other wanes."

"Cause and effect."

"In part. It's surely more than that, you have the idea. The Holy Spirit is moving strongly in this city with Persis Magen's evangelistic campaign. Almost palpably. You see miracles on every side."

"Therefore the unholy spirit is hard at work as well. In what way? Undoing the miracles?"

"No. God's Word does not return void. His miracles cannot be undone. Brother Larry feels, and I'm certain he's correct, that Satan's only recourse is to damage or destroy the evangelistic campaign itself."

"By smearing it with the taint of crime."

"Exactly! Well phrased. Also, by removing key persons."

Joe stared at Tommy simply because Tommy sat in his line of sight. Tommy stared back, his ear to his phone, eavesdropping. Joe pressed on. "Does Brother Larry—do you yourself—believe Persis Magen is a target?"

"Oh, she's always been a target of Satan. Every effective believer is."

"Of the bomber?"

Another pause. "I can't begin to guess Satan's intents and purposes. Discernment of spirits is not one of my spiritual gifts. However, in 2 Corinthians—Brother Larry quoted it this morning—it tells how Satan would not have crucified Jesus

Christ if he had known Christ would overcome death thereby. In other words, God uses Satan's mischief for His good."

Joe picked up the ball. "And this latest bit of mischief, this murder and attempted murder, is going to be used for God's purposes."

" 'Used to God's glory,' to quote Brother Larry exactly."

"I see. And where do I fit in—I and all these phone calls?"

"Either you are for God and Jesus, or you're working for Satan. There is no neutral ground. You're obviously not working in God's behalf, because you're on the verge of arresting Persis Magen, which would end her campaign prematurely and play right into Satan's hands."

"Why do you say I am about to accuse her? Did your Brother Larry mention evidence, or hearsay, in his commentary, that would point the police toward Persis Magen?"

"Well, no; he didn't say anything like that specifically."

"Read between the lines of his comments for me a moment. Do you see any channels of inquiry we might pursue, any interviews that might bear fruit?"

Silence on the line. She obviously was thinking about it. "No, not really. And I'm not sure I'd tell you if I did."

"I understand Jesus Christ is strongly identified with truth. We're trying to find the truth about these crimes."

"Then why did you say on television that you

were arresting Persis Magen?"

Now what? Joe racked his memory and came up with zip. "I said no such thing, Mrs. Crane. My only TV exposure on this case was a twenty-second bite when a KOOL team ambushed me late yesterday. I mentioned nothing about filing charges of any sort then."

More silence on the other end. "I'm certain Brother Larry would never lie or distort the facts."

"If he obtained this information secondhand, he may not have been the one who distorted the facts. But they're distorted, nonetheless."

"I'm sorry. No. I can't believe Brother Larry would allow distortion. I would like to believe you, Mr. Rodriguez. You're an articulate and intelligent man. But a little voice keeps reminding me that Satan disguises himself as an angel of light."

Joe chuckled. "You just equated someone who respects English with angels. My mother would be absolutely delighted. And so, Mrs. Crane, your Brother Larry is urging all his listeners to mount a telephone campaign to keep Satan at bay."

"If Satan wins this one, it won't be because the true believers are sitting on their hands."

Tommy punched his phone onto another line. He purred into it and his face froze. He shot an undecipherable gesture to Joe.

"Mrs. Crane, my partner just informed me we have something on the front burner. I must go. Again, I appreciate your help immensely. Now I understand better what's happening. Thank you very much."

A few more words passed between them and she

hung up.

Brother Larry. Protest. Satan's minions. Joe was beginning to regret this case even more, and the luck of the draw which had dumped it in his lap—rather, Jerry, his lieutenant, who dumped it in his lap.

Brother Larry. Another foaming-at-the-mouth religious freak. Joe carefully avoided strong involvement in religion. It wasn't his interest. In fact, it made him uneasy. All these religious fanatics of every persuasion, Eastern and Western, and all of them dead sure they're right and everyone else is wrong—he didn't want to get involved in any of that. Now, here he was, a simple cop who loved mysteries and hated metaphysics, up to his ears in the stuff. Misquoted by some radical shepherd of some flock who . . . aw, nuts! A policeman's lot is not a happy one.

"I look forward to an intense chat with Brother Larry." Joe pointed to Tommy's phone. "What's on?"

"'Twas our esteemed lieutenant on the other line. And to quote exactly: He wants to know what bozo gave some irate eighty-year-old maniac his card."

STEEL SOPRANO

So this was Jules Robinson. Like Harry Wallace and other tall people, he could probably eat like the proverbial horse and never gain an ounce. Joe sat in a corner booth with his cola and watched Jules bite into his second extraburger. The last vestiges of a clear, red Arizona sundown were tinting the west window.

Joe didn't want to automatically despise the young man. That wasn't professional. But with this guy it came naturally. Jules' hands were soft and effeminate, his hips and thighs unusually heavy, his shoulders disproportionately narrow. Just what were his sexual proclivities, Joe wondered. It didn't matter to him professionally, but it could figure heavily in the case. Fundamentalists come down hard on homosexuality and Persis was as fundamental as you get. It just might matter. On the other hand, Jules might be straight as a plumbline. Joe's headache had disappeared with his nap. Now it was back.

Jules used a pinky finger to poke an errant strand of shredded lettuce back into his mouth. "About a year and a half."

"What?"

"You asked when I came to work for Persis. About a year and a half. September a year ago."

"At her meetings in Hartford."

"Yes. No, not exactly. It was there I first met her. She showed me the need of a Savior in my life. She brought me to the foot of the cross."

Why can't preacher types speak plain English? "But you hired into the organization later."

"Yes. No, not exactly. I'm not hired as such. You see, I'm an accountant. A very fine accountant. I could be a CPA if I wanted to, very easily. I knew she needed me. God told me she needed me. So I just kept reminding her until she remembered to heed God and accept my ministry. She fights God sometimes, you know. Resists the Holy Spirit."

Joe thought the word *pestered* fit nicely here. "She pays you a wage, or what? You said not hired as such."

"She pays my expenses when we're on the road, which is several times a year, but I actually work for her full time. It's a ministry. I have other income."

"Tom says you travel ahead and set up accommodations, untangle last-minute knots, that sort of thing. You were in Riverside yesterday?"

"Drove back to Phoenix here last night. I prefer to drive at night. Less crowded on the freeway. Got

in this morning a few hours after dawn. The desert
wildflowers are superb this year, aren't they? I understand they don't bloom well every year. Only
years with enough rainfall. Is that right?"

"That's right. I notice a lot of poppies and lupine
out beyond Mesa, toward Apache Junction. And the
Superstitions usually put on a good show." Joe
paused a moment, thinking. "The color should be
especially nice around Yuma too. Was it?"

"Yuma? Yes. Yes it was. Delightful."

"You drive the company car. Persis and the others fly from city to city."

"Correct. Coach too. Precious doll, Persis. Always
ready to save a dollar for the Lord. That's good
stewardship, you know." He wallowed a french fry
around in his catsup and popped it into his mouth.

"Why didn't they fly from Albuquerque to
Phoenix?"

"Persis had an engagement in—I forget the name.
Not meetings; a visit with an old friend, some retired
fellow. Show Me. Showplace. Something."

"Show Low?"

"That's it. A gentleman in Albuquerque provided
them one of his rentals. Persis reads in the car,
writes her messages. She doesn't get car sick, not
even on winding roads. So she redeems the time,
you see. It's not wasted."

"I assume when you drive, you stick to shortline
distance? Save mileage?"

"Of course."

"So they took I-40 west through Gallup and
down. And you took I-8 directly to Riverside and
back."

"Right. It's a long drive." He polished off his fries.

"And when they don't have free access to a car, they just sort of make-do while you're off lining up the next gig."

"Gig?"

"Engagement. Series of meetings."

"Correct. Now that car that blew up, they knew nothing about it when they accepted it. You just can't trust the quality of rentals. I hope, from this, that Persis will decide to bring two cars on the road. I've been urging that for some time."

Now what was the best approach? Joe sifted mentally through various methods of extracting unusual bits of information and decided on hostility. If Jules Robinson was as soft as he looked, a little macho indignation should work wonders.

"Mr. Robinson. You know and I know how Cat Dubois died, and yet you try to make me think you believe her car exploded spontaneously. I don't like being diddled like that. Especially when you're so inept at diddling."

Jules' mouth dropped open. Bits of mangled french fries peeked out.

Joe pressed it. "Where were you yesterday, Mr. Robinson? The truth this time."

"Riverside! I can prove it. The arrangements are all set up. And I got Persis some very good rates too. Call the Vacation House Motel. They'll tell you."

"We will. Now let's discuss your relationship with Cat DuBois. I mean the real relationship, not what Persis thinks."

"Marie shouldn't have said anything! It wasn't true. There was nothing dirty between us."

"We didn't get it from Marie. Other sources. I told you I don't like being diddled. Now you can cooperate here, or we can go downtown and talk to a polygraph."

"You can't put me on a lie detector without my permission. I know my rights."

"We'll get your permission. In writing." Here was an accountant—a very uptight, defensive accountant—who kept mentioning the cost of things. Joe fired a wild, wild shot into the dark. "How much money, exactly, was involved in your relationship with Cat? How much changed hands?"

Jules turned white. Fear? Hatred? His lips drew a tight, almost seamless line across his face. Hatred. He exuded hatred as a garbage truck exudes odor. Unmistakable hatred. Why did he feel cornered? Joe must be careful now to press in the right direction.

Jules didn't give him time for another question. The gangly accountant hissed, "You keep your black nose out of my business!" He slid out of the seat and hurried away. He almost tripped a little girl on his way out the door into the darkness.

Joe sighed and sat back to sort this out. So much for the hostility approach. Red taillights pulled out of the parking lot, nearly colliding with traffic. There went his ride. They had come in Jules' car; rather, Persis' car, Jules at the wheel. Joe fished in his pocket for a quarter and walked back to the phones.

Three rings. Either Sammie the dispatcher was

very busy or she was doing her nails and the polish was wet.

"Police." Sammie's sexy voice promised much and never betrayed the fact that at five-feet-four she weighed 232 pounds.

"Hi, Sammie. Joe. Give me Henrietta, please."

"Henrietta it is. They tell me you really blew your cool last night on a real hot date."

"That's four. And Sammie? Send a black and white around to the Extraburger at Camelback and Forty-Fourth. I need a ride."

"Sure. Carl's in that area and he breaks in a few minutes. You'll probably have to buy him a hot dog. Only four? The department's slipping."

Rhythmic beeps.

"Records, Nieswonger."

"Henny? Joe. I'd like to know if a Jules Robinson or anyone close to that flew from Phoenix to Riverside and back in the last few days. Would have arrived back at Sky Harbor today or yesterday, probably."

"Standard records check in the bargain?"

"If Tom hasn't done it already. Look at the sheet first."

"Spell it."

"R-O-B-I-N-S-O-N, Jules."

"Hark. A computer speaks. I'll leave it in your basket. Say, you're going to have to take me out on a date sometime. I hear when you and a girl are in a motel, the fireworks really fly."

"Everybody's Bob Hope. I'll check my basket in the morning."

Five.

Joe arrived at the motel twenty minutes before Persis, Marie, and Tom. No Jules. He spent the time with Chen, watching the motel from across the alley and being enlightened about spring training and the upcoming baseball season.

Cat DuBois' wake arrived, spearheaded by an Irishman. Apparently the meeting had gone exceedingly well. Persis was joy-filled. Tom exuberant, Marie almost bubbly. Almost. The women trooped inside.

Tom paused by Joe. "How'd it go with Jules? I need a pack."

Joe dug for the cigarettes. "Blew it. Tried to browbeat him and chased him off instead."

"Eh, can't win 'em all."

"Did pull one little goody. Asked him about Yuma and I-8. He says the flowers are just delightful along there."

"But I-8 doesn't go to Riverside. I-10 does. Aha! Fly to Riverside, do your business, fly back. Then use the extra time pursuing skulduggery, whilst no one knows ye be in town." Tom shook out a cigarette.

"Hennie's checking plane manifests. I'll call Vacation House Motel tomorrow and find out exactly when and how he made his arrangements."

"How about I call the motel and yourself check credit cards. He'd have to buy gas on the road. Or would he pay cash?" Tom turned his back to the warm and sullen breeze to light up.

"You gonna torch that off and carry it inside?"

Tom studied his cigarette thoughtfully and put it away. "These people are making an honest man of me."

"Perish the thought. Who's on duty?"

"Turk and Harley should be relieving Chen in fifteen minutes." Tom turned toward the motel room. "Go home and get some more sleep. I'm going to directly."

"Which reminds me. Thanks for the nap this morning, but you shouldn't have."

"Meself would love to take credit, but 'twas Marie's idea. We unplugged the phone and sat about the pool."

"Learn anything?" Joe had every intention of climbing into his MG and driving home. Instead his feet ambled off toward the motel room.

"Aye. Meself has learned never to become famous. People were staring at us, a few came up for autographs and this one young fellow with a Bible was determined to set her straight on the truth about when the world's ending. Which, by the way, is in less than two years, so you'd best get your tires paid off."

"If the end's that soon, I'll take out another charge card. What else've you learned?"

"Persis never gave the least hint she was dissatisfied with Cat. I couldn't fire 'em too close to center with Marie sitting there—we should hit the ladies separately with that one—but Persis gave the impression that she thinks Cat was clean as a surgical tray." Tom crossed the last twenty feet to the motel room in silence, knocked, paused and stepped inside.

"Interesting." Joe smiled at the ladies. "You two look like you just got off the world's greatest merry-go-round."

Persis put both hands on Joe's arms and squeezed. "I wish you'd been there. In fact, I had you two in mind when I put the message together."

"I'm flattered. You don't happen to have it in print?"

"It just happens I do!" Jubilant as a knight victorious, she snapped her briefcase open on the bed and started riffling.

"Some excellent points she made, Joe." Tom closed the refrigerator door, a fried chicken leg in his hand. "She says ye can't buy your way into heaven with good deeds. Good deeds cannot blot out the bad ones. Only blood buys ye out. Right?"

"Very good, Mr. Flaherty."

"And I've one or two to me credit." His brogue was getting thicker. Either he was finally getting tired or he was still putting on a show for Marie. Joe couldn't decide which.

"Sorry I missed it." Joe ought to encourage this religion business, much as it irritated him. Religion fuels wars and drives nations; it could well prod murder. It looked as if Tom thought along the same line. What should Joe ask next?

"Not to worry, detective." Persis handed him a neat, handwritten three-pager. "I just happen to have the text here. Jesus paid with His lifeblood for every wrong thing ever done; yours, mine, those of our Irish dervish here." Her voice dropped a peg. "Cat's too. Perfect payment for offense against a perfect God. Marie, you are bobbing up and down."

Marie spread her hands helplessly. "I'm restless. I wish Jules were back with the car. Where did he go, anyway? I want to drive somewhere. Do something. Get something. I can't sit."

Joe heard change jingle in Tom's pocket. "Call it," said Tom.

"Heads."

The coin *fwapped* in Tom's hand. "Best two of three."

"Tails."

Fwap. "Ye peeked, ye blackguard!"

Joe held out a hand to Marie. "Remember, Tom. Duck behind the counter if Persis decides to shower. We'll be back before too long." He ushered Marie out the door.

It had worked *so* smoothly, this separation of the women. He permitted himself a smug little smile.

They walked out across the lot as Turk and Harley arrived for their stint as protectors of Persis Magen. Joe waved and spoke and held the Midget's passenger door for her.

"What a cute little car!" With her slight build, she was one of the few adults who fit with room to spare. "Do you know every man on the force?"

He squirmed behind the wheel. "Naa. Used to, once. Where to?"

"I don't care. Pick up some treat for Persis, and for Jules when he gets back."

"Sounds good." He gunned the motor.

She flinched.

He wheeled it streetside and watched for a hole to slip into.

"Guess I'm gun-shy." She draped a lovely arm over the open window.

"Don't blame you. How close were you and Cat anyway?" They jackrabbited out into traffic. Where

were all these cars coming from? Regional basketball finals. That was it.

"It's hard to explain." She leaned back and let
the wind tug her hair. "Cat was burned so many
times she plastered this tough shell around herself.
Wouldn't even let Persis in, not really. Two failed
marriages, a couple sour shack-ups. And what was
she, thirty? Maybe not quite that. I didn't try to
become close. I contented myself with being helpful. 'Supportive' is the word, I suppose. We all
were. Except Jules."

"What was Jules?"

"In love. Oh, he was a gentleman; she gave him
no choice. But his idea of heaven was marrying
Cat. You've met him. You can see she'd have some
trouble warming to the idea."

"I like your way with words. Cat was black. Light
black, but black. I got the definite impression he's a
racist. Isn't that contradictory?"

"Jules is all contradictions. He called you black
too, right?"

"Now that you mention it."

She giggled. "He called some little Korean gentleman black once too. The poor man just stood
there blinking." She twisted in her seat and tucked
a leg under. "I don't think Jules actually believes
he's superior or anything because he's white. He's
not a supremist. He just has this way of categoriz-
ing the whole human race. Either you're blond like
him or you're black. So he's racist, but he's not."
She frowned at Joe. "See what I mean?"

"I can see where he could cause a lot of problems. There's a good deal of public relations to Per-

sis' operation. Doesn't he ever embarrass the organization when he calls every Tomas, Ricardo, and Harry-hito black?"

"Oh, he's much better than he used to be. He's matured immensely since Persis took him under her wing. She even ..."

"Really?"

"Oh, my yes. You should have met him a year ago. You know, he's really very bright in his own way. Doesn't relate well, but he's smart."

"I've heard that elsewhere too." Joe glanced again at the rearview mirror.

"Where are we going?"

"There are three very nice lovers' lanes around Phoenix. South Mountain Park, but that's twenty-five miles away. Camelback Mountain. And an economy model across Papago Park toward Tempe. I thought I'd take you up Camelback a little way and show you the city lights."

"Now wait a minute, *Mr.* Rodriguez."

"Strictly business, I promise. No monkeyshines. Besides, I'm interrogating you, in case you didn't notice."

"Yes, I did notice. I assumed you're one of those workaholics who can't forget business. How many people do you talk to in a day?"

"Never kept track. Usually thirty or forty in the course of any one investigation."

She glanced back. "You think someone is following us?"

"Possibly."

"You can't tell in this traffic. Look at the head-lights."

"You're right. I'm just naturally suspicious." He made a few unusual turns and jogs. He tried to keep the conversation going, more specifically to explore what Marie knew of the team's finances and Cat's past. Was Persis satisfied with Cat's work? With her lifestyle? Yes and Yes. But he couldn't keep his mind on both jobs successfully, quizzing and driving. Possibly there was a car behind them, occasionally switching lanes, sometimes far behind, sometimes closer. It never moved in close enough for him to get a make on it. Or maybe he was keeping track of a dozen innocent pairs of headlights.

Now they were cruising residential streets. Low rambling houses with enough floor space to cover a football field tucked themselves behind palms and orange trees and transplanted saguaro cactus. He shifted down to third and started up the mountain. Apparently he was suspicious in vain. No headlights followed, although the mountain curves were too tight to be sure.

She was watching behind as closely as he. "I don't see any lights. I think we're alone. No monkeyshines, huh?"

"Naw. I'll let Tom make the first pass. He has this delightful line that's long enough to hang wash on. You'll love it."

She was about to make some indignant retort. Instead she said, "Ooooooooooooh." Four hundred and fifty square miles of twinkling lights stretched to the horizon in two directions.

"It gets better farther up. Try the radio. There's an easy-listening station somewhere around 84."

"I thought all cops had CB so you could talk to each other. And all the TV cops have car phones." She flicked it on.

"Tom says I oughta. The way I see it, they can reach me at home, they can reach me at work, they can reach me in the company car. This is one place they can leave me alone."

"I hear a ring of possessiveness in your voice when you talk about your car."

"You hear right."

No headlights behind. He must have been wrong. She toyed with the radio a little. The dial light and sound both flickered. The station cut in and out.

"Nuts."

"What am I doing wrong, Joe?"

"Nothing. There's this little wire back underneath. Someday I'm going to heat up the soldering iron, crawl back there and stick it on right. I repair it temporarily by crimping it against its connection with my fingernail and a piece of tape. Takes two people to hold and crimp and stick." Usually he admitted freely the reduced use of his right arm and right leg. He had come to terms with the permanence of his loss. He was past it, right? So why couldn't he mention it to this pretty lady? What was so special about her that he regressed in so basic a matter?

"How long is 'temporarily'?"

"Oh, fifteen, eighteen months at a time."

"I safety-pin hems in the same way. Temporarily. Funny how time flies."

There were no other cars in this scenic pullout. The basketball fans must still be moaning and cheering elsewhere. Joe swung a tight 180 and parked near the edge. A zillion lights spread out forever.

They were not alone after all. Another set of headlights came up from below and passed on by without altering speed.

He opened the door on his side, extricated his legs and hung them outside. He shoved the shift lever up into third to give himself more room and twisted around.

"I thought you said no monkeyshines."

"I also said it takes two people to fix this thing. Scrunch down and hold this wire under here. Farther back. Feel it?"

She buckled her long legs and crunched into a knot, groping beneath the dash. "Oh. That one. I thought you said 'little.' "

As he folded up and twisted, the better to angle his left arm up under the radio, headlights from behind them glinted off the windshield rim. The back of his neck prickled.

Backfires resemble gunshots, but gunshots are unmistakable. His windshield perforated where their heads had been a moment ago.

Without thinking he scooted face up out the door into the warm gravel. He vaguely remembered yelling at her to stay down—or was it only that he intended to? He was out of the car, head down and rolling across the loose stones.

An engine revved. Headlights came hurtling toward them. The crazy driver was going to smash right into his MG, send everything over the side at once. A hundred feet of steep bank fell away beyond his right tires. He was stupid to park out in the open here! Major league stupid!

He came up on one knee and steadied his gun with both hands. Apparently intimidated, the headlights veered left and out onto the road. This was no time to think about internal affairs investigations six months down the road. He shot to kill.

He heard the windshield go but he must not have hit the driver. The car slammed past them. Three shots left. He lowered his aim to try for tires. Before the car careened out of sight around the curve, he put out at least one tire and a taillight.

Joe had the motor running before he was fully in the seat. The wheels howled in the loose gravel. They left the burnt-rubber smell behind. He realized belatedly he was driving with gun in hand.

How was he going to reload and drive? Essentially toothless, here he was, bearing down on an eager assassin.

"Joe, all the holes are on my side of the windshield! He tried to shoot *me!*"

"Maybe. Maybe he figured if we were parking, I'd be on your side, too. I have a few enemies socked away here and there."

"You mean this isn't the person who. . . ? I mean isn't connected to Cat?"

There he was, just ahead; one taillight out, jerking and weaving, driving on a rim.

"Bombers and shooters usually don't mix. Some psycho theory on premeditation versus hot blood."

He was closing quickly—too quickly. He hated to try to force the vehicle off this curving road. What if some innocent driver came along as he pulled into the uphill lane?

Ever so briefly he saw the one brakelight left in the car ahead. He stood on the brakes as the vehicle came swinging around broadside, blocking both lanes. Just barely in time he managed to bring his own back and around. Steel on steel shrieked in ultrasoprano as his beloved MG collided side-on with his quarry.

MUCKMIND

Marie stood close by Tom's left side and watched her employer step to the lectern. Perhaps Persis was right. Perhaps Marie should go back to Waukesha until this ghastly business was resolved. Her nerves were shot, but that was only natural. Think how shot Joe's nerves must be. It was his MG, not hers. She wished he were here now to hear Persis' message.

Persis wove a lovely extended illustration around Romans 8:28, but she didn't stop there. Who is the recipient of the promise? That is, who is the lucky person who fits both qualifications — a lover of God and one called for His purposes? Marie watched Tom closely. How deeply was he comprehending? She couldn't tell. Where was Joe now?

In a few moments Persis would call forward those who would claim eternal life by surrendering to

Jesus. If Tom stepped forward, Marie would feel so happy to follow at his side, to be his personal counselor. If only there were no distractions now!

Movement rustled at Tom's right. It was Joe.

Tom whispered, "Wrecked any good cars lately?"

Joe answered, "Cruel, good buddy. Vicious. Who's on the dais? Hello, Marie."

She smiled and nodded. How could she tell Joe Rodriguez that he ought to be listening and responding to the message?

"Harry and Sherm. We've tightened up since last night. If the cad's decided to switch from bombs to bullets, he could come from anywhere."

Joe nodded. "If last night was connected to this case at all. I still think it could be one of Louie's people."

"Then ye might's well cancel that honeymoon to Siberia. If it's Louie, you're dead, me brawny lad."

"You sure are a bucket of cheer tonight."

"Mail call depresses me."

"What does that mean?"

Tom grimaced. "Persis got another crank note, about like the third. Halfway down the stack of mail Jules brought in. No postmark, so it didn't go through the post office."

"So the clown's too cheap to put a stamp on it."

Tom snorted. "Probably waiting till the post office has a sale on them. Gretchen's examining fingerprints and such, but we've scant hope of finding anything."

"How many people had access to Persis' mail stack?"

"Every fair soul in Arizona and probably a few

others . . . Ah, here we go." Tom pointed toward the dais.

Persis was stepping down into the crowd. Tom slipped around to Marie's left. With Joe at her right the three of them moved forward. This wasn't the way she wanted them to be joining the churning mass of new believers. These two were all business, alert and serious, watching everywhere, oblivious to the meaning of the occasion or to the words being spoken.

Tom and Joe and two others seemed especially anxious to spirit Persis away tonight. Against their best efforts, though, the pastor in charge of follow-up in the Peoria area collared Persis for five minutes of earnest conversation. Marie had always thought Peoria was in Illinois, but this hellish state must have one too. She had been uncomfortably warm all day. The detectives scowled and chafed and shifted from foot to foot. Finally they all hustled down a tunnel and out a back door.

Joe stopped by a black and white police cruiser at the door. "Mrs. Magen, you invited the boys to late dinner a couple nights ago. Would you do me a favor and feed Harry and Sherm here?"

"I'd be delighted. Just two?"

Joe smiled. "Tom and I will go along back with Marie."

Persis nodded sagely. "Fine. Where would you like to eat, gentlemen?"

One man poked Joe and whispered hoarsely, "Who's paying?"

"You fight it out."

Joe held the passenger door open for Marie. She

slid inside and he disappeared. He got in the driver's side and settled behind the wheel.

This was not one of those police cars built like a cage in the back seat. No wire screen, no shotgun bolted in the front seat. On the outside it looked official; in here, it looked like any other out-of-date sedan.

"Rocinante!" Tom boomed. "Can't be! Sure'n they junked this sorry crate months ago." He came plopping into the seat beside Marie. He slammed the door once, twice, three times. The latch caught. "Ah, just like old times!"

"Rocinante?" Marie frowned. "Wasn't that Don Quixote's bony old horse?"

Tom grinned as the car moved forward. "When Joe made detective, some of the old-liners who weren't quite ready for such an event called Joe Don Quixote, out to tilt at the windmills of social repression and all. A derogatory sort of name, if ye catch me drift. I played Sancho Panza to Joe's Don. This was our car, good old 317668. Ah, many's the time I wrote that number on a trip ticket. We were the joke of the force. Then one darlin' morning, it dawned on the bosses that we had a 96 percent conviction rate. They still call Joe the Don now and again, but they tip their hats whilst saying it."

"An Irish Sancho Panza." Marie giggled, then paused. "You're awfully quiet, Mr. Quixote. But then I don't blame you. Did the insurance adjuster see your car yet?"

"This afternoon. If the frame's sprung we scrap it. Otherwise, down three weeks. Maybe four."

"And who's the proud owner of the vehicle that

kissed yours so lightly?" Tom pulled his cigarettes, looked at them a moment and put them away.

"Easy Rent-a-Car out of Sky Harbor. A portly fellow—five-eight, about 250—arrived at the airport around 7 P.M. from Atlanta. Signed out a rental and picked up his luggage. When he reached in his pocket the car key was gone. He can't remember being jostled or approached by anyone, suspicious looking or otherwise. So he went back to the desk for another car. I spent half an hour checking on him. He's clean."

"What a lovely scam. Hang about the desk, pick the pocket of the luckless traveler who just rented a car for you, and drive off to do mayhem. So the unsuccessful marksman found his niche as a pickpocket. Good. Perhaps now he'll let you alone and stick with the trade he does best."

"Fat chance. I doubt our bomber/shootist is all that light-fingered. Probably hired the job out. You can buy a dip for a bottle of wine."

"Every time I see a silver lining, Jose, yourself points out the cloud. Speaking of clouds, we checked out all the other cars in the motel parking lot at bomb time. Nothing. Apparently the bomber did his work on the correct vehicle. There be a Scottsdale businessman who's certain, though, that I'm a private eye in the employ of his wife. Considers me a splendid forger in the bargain to be able to trump up such a dandy imitation of police ID."

Marie watched the headlights come and go on all sides. How did Joe know last night that one set of thousands followed them? Police officers must have some special sense for that sort of thing. She realized too that when the TV news said police were investigating a certain heinous crime, these were the men alluded to.

Tom filled Joe in on the message — "homily" he called it. Not only had he absorbed it all, he had it all straight. He even applied it to Joe: of course, crunching your beloved car is discouraging, but there must be some good thing to come of it. Joe wasn't buying. Marie hated to see him so obviously depressed.

Rocinante's suspension system matched that of a decrepit nag. They jolted over the speed bump in the motel lot hard enough to lift her off the seat. The brakes made moaning protest noises as they pulled up in front of the room.

Inside, Tom flicked on the light and marched directly to the refrigerator. Joe motioned Marie toward one of the padded chairs.

She sat. "Aren't you going to check through drawers for bombs?"

Joe pulled a chair around and sat across from her. He leaned forward, his elbows on his knees. "We have a twenty-four-hour watch on the room." Then his dark, dark eyes bored into hers. "Two years ago you threatened to kill Persis Magen."

She gasped, not from fear but from surprise. "I'd forgotten that. I'd honestly forgotten all about it. Hey, now wait just a minute! You don't think... you do, don't you!"

"The note number three that you so conveniently hauled out of the wastebasket came out of Cat's typewriter, a machine you have access to. Since Cat's machine is in our lab and the fourth arrived today, you must have written all four at once so you could salt them into the mail pile now and then. Which spells premeditation. Mad bombers are natural premeditators; comes in the package. Is this the time, Marie? Have you let your first threat, made in anger, cool off enough that no one would suspect you now? These things can fester a long time, you know."

Marie snapped around toward Tom. Surely he could talk some sense into Joe. Tom stood open-mouthed, staring. Obviously this was all new to him. She turned back to Joe. "Look. I'm sorry your little car got kiboshed, but you don't have to take it out on me. I didn't really know her two years ago. I was mad. Angry. Not now . You're nuts if you think I'd hurt her. Or Cat either."

"You threatened to get Persis if it took you thirty years."

So he was going to persist with this. Marie sat back and sighed. "Yes, I believe that was the figure I quoted. Who did you get it from?"

"You had good reason. Persis dumped on you. Turned you in."

"I suppose you could call it that, but it's not true. What she did was best for me. I know that now."

"Enlighten me." Tom plopped down on a stool and licked strawberry jam off his fingers.

"Marie here was a working woman at fifteen. Nothing fancy. Just the streets. Supported herself, her pimp, and her habit for two or three years. She was pregnant and mainlining when she stumbled into one of Persis' meetings. Came to Persis privately to ask for spiritual help. Persis turned her in, signed her into a hospital, and effectively prevented her from obtaining an abortion."

"Everything she did was right. I thank God for her."

"Incidentally, remember Mrs. Bachmeyer, your counselor at the shelter for unwed mothers? She's director now. Thought you might like to know your friends are getting up in the world. You tried twice to commit suicide before the baby arrived and you turned on Persis with a razor blade when she came to visit you. After that you changed face, became a pussycat. Biding your time, right? Waiting. Flow with it since you can't change anything anyway, and wait. You'd have plenty of time later to get her, after she paid all the bills."

"That visit by Persis was when I truly accepted Jesus Christ as my Savior. I gave it all over to Him then. Yes, I slashed her with a razor blade. She still has a little bit of a white mark on her arm. There she was, bleeding like crazy, and she wasn't even mad. She kept loving me even when I did that to her. It's the first time anyone ever showed me what love means."

"Love. Doesn't take you long to come out of mourning, does it. Crocodile tears one night and the next night you're bouncing around like a Kewpie doll on a rubber band."

"Why me? Why are you doing this to me?"

"You had access to the typewriter. You know the operation. You also know something about explosives and probably have access to them also; your pimp in Milwaukee was a Nam vet experienced in everything from plastiques to black powder. You were . . ."

"How do you know all this garbage? How can you sit there and spew out. . . ?"

"I spent all morning on the phone. Don't waste your fancy line on her, Tom. Just wave a dollar bill."

"I'm innocent!"

"You're very good at creating an impression of innocence. You really had me fooled. That 'no monkeyshines' business last night, for instance. Pure, self-righteous little nun."

His attitude wasn't new; she dealt with it all the time. Why did it bother her so now? Some snooty church member learns about her past and tells her she's not welcome there anymore. An upstanding businessman hears about her and hits on her. Big deal. So why did Joe hurt her so deeply? She didn't know and didn't care. And she wasn't going to sit here and smile about it, either.

She straightened to meet him eye to eye. "You're right I was a pro, and I was good too. I know more ways to please a customer than you'll ever dream of for fixing a radio. Hookers don't forget, let me tell you. But God forgets. He promised. Once He forgives, it's blotted out.

"I love the way you toss the word 'self-righteous' around, Quixote. Obviously once a pig wallows in the mud you figure it's never clean again. Well, it happens I am clean. Not a pop, not a single man, since I made that commitment to God and to Persis Magen. She showed me what life is. I have a purpose and I have complete forgiveness. I'm a new woman. God doesn't remember my past. If you choose to, that's your problem. I'm clear, you two-bit muckmind. Free and clear on all counts."

She jumped up and started for the door. His left arm whipped out and grabbed hers. "I'm not finished with you."

She slapped his hand aside. "You're never going to get started with me, Quixote. Stick it in your windmill." She wrenched the door open, slammed it behind her, let the cool night air try to soothe her face. It didn't. She saw in the shadows one of the policemen assigned to watch the room. He stepped back out of sight.

Why? Why did she let Joe get to her? The door clicked behind her. It was Tom, not Joe. The Irishman called, "Don't get a silly little notion like running. Unwise, lass."

She didn't slow her march across the parking lot. He came jogging up and fell in beside her, matching her stride for stride. "I hate to say it, lass, but he's got enough to arrest ye on suspicion should he care to. So you'd best just stick around and ride it out."

"I don't need any advice, Flaherty. Or any favors, either. If I'm out to get Persis, why did I let Cat climb in with the bomb?"

"A hypothetical situation. A cares a great deal about B. C hates A and doesn't give a donkey's breakfast for B. So C hurts B just to spite A. Then C hurts A as well. Twice the pain, ye see, emotional and physical, and the victims be hanged. Happens now and again. Or mayhap Cat was the intended victim for reasons unbeknownst to us." Tom bobbed his shoulders. "If it makes ye feel better, lass, I believe ye."

"It doesn't. And you can get off the phony accent. I'm not impressed."

" 'Tis no phony, my dear colleen. Took me most of me adult life to shed it. The straight talk—the Americanese, if you will—that's me phony accent."

"Why me? I think Cat had some sort of past, though neither she nor Persis ever told me anything about it. Jules certainly does. Why is Joe coming down so hard on me?"

They had reached the far end of the parking lot. She could choose now between climbing over the low cinder-block wall or sitting on it. She sat.

Tom perched a few feet away and tucked one knee up under his chin. "There be a technique of interviewing wherein ye make as though you're the injured party; incensed at something, sore disappointed, whatever. By which, then, ye extract information—sometimes, rarely even a confession—you'd never hope to get by more casual means. Joe tries it every now and then and it always backfires for him. An interrogator he's not. A brilliant investigator he is, though. How he dredges up the goodies so fast nor so thoroughly I've never understood. If he spent the morning on the phone, you'd best believe he can tell ye what ye had for breakfast three years ago last March."

"I'm so happy he's a success in his field."

"That's why we work together so well, ye see. We complement each other, being I make up what he lacks and vice the versa. He claims meself could wangle the hydrogen bomb formula out of a parking meter and I believe him. I've worked some minor miracles talking to suspects."

"Certainly glad to see you're not conceited."

"Conceited? Not at all, lass. I know what I can do and I'm proud of how well I do it. That's honest evaluation, not conceit. But ye see, I've an edge on Joe. He's not much good at reading people, which is the gift required to succeed as an interrogator. He can't much see through me, but I can read him like the daily racing form. He cares warmly about ye, lass."

"Oh sure. It's written all over him."

"And ye pegged him right on the nose. Self-righteous. As I was saying a moment ago, he's not much good at faking an air of indignation—or disappointment. Tonight was real. He's leaning on ye because he's found ye to be a prime suspect in this mess and he's sore disappointed. Consternated."

"Tough apples. I've had my fill of hypocrites."

"Hypocrite? Joe? Oh, no, lass! He's done his best his whole life to stay straight and honest and responsible and good to the world. A rare quality in a cop these days, I assure ye. We tend to grow cynical in our old age. And he has more than his share of reasons to be sour on the world."

Tom shifted on his perch. "His kids are, let's see, around six and nine now. They live with his sister and her three. He and his sister share the raising of all five. When the oldest was born, still in diapers— the boy, Rico—his wife ran off in a van with some bearded fellow. Wore camouflage, he did. A real loony. Claimed she wanted to find herself. Joe found her and brought her home and forgave her.

"She swore never again. When the little girl, Gloria, was a year old she ran off same as before, this time with a fellow in a pinstripe suit. Fantastic lover, I suppose, but a lousy driver. Ran his car over a cement bridge abutment and into the crosscut canal. They both drowned. Joe pretty much swore off women. Spends his time taking the kids to the zoo and waxing his MG."

"He must have loved his wife a great deal."

Tom's voice purred gently. "He still does."

Persis' car pulled into the lot and stopped at the far side. Jules got out and she could see even from this distance that he was in one of his black snits. He disappeared into his room.

Tom reached back to the tall, thick hedge behind the cinder-block wall and plucked a white blossom. He twirled it about between his fingers. "Oleanders. Lovely, eh? But poisonous. Joe wouldn't admit it, of course, but I can see he was softening up toward ye there. He's starting to come out of his shell, but being so bloody slow about it. I was hoping you'd do him some good."

"Tom, when the two of you flipped a coin last night, remember? Did he really win the toss, or was that your shrewd little attempt at matchmaking?"

"You'll never know, lass." The smokey eyes twinkled.

"Tom!" Joe's voice bellowed across the lot. He was standing in the doorway. He closed the door behind him. "I'm leaving. Come, if you want a ride." Casually he tossed himself into Rocinante's driver's seat and waited, one foot still on the ground.

Marie stood up. Her backside felt sore and

squared-off, a negative image of the rough cinder-block. She started back slowly, Tom close to her side.

Tom purred, "Ye mentioned a while ago that Jules certainly has some sort of unsavory past, but we've found no police record on him at all. Would ye care to elaborate on that?"

"He has a history of unbalanced acts. Irrational acts. Surely an investigator as sharp as Joe would have found it by now. Jules used to be very boastful about the weird things he had done. Truly weird things. He pretty much quit boasting, though, these last three or four months. Part of growing up, I guess."

They passed Rocinante. Even though the motel room door stood already ajar, Tom gallantly held it for her. "See ye on the morrow, lass."

She stepped inside. The moment the door closed she pressed her ear against the crack. Tom said something about Jules. She heard Joe's voice, "Sounds like she's pointing the finger of suspicion any direction but herself. Any old . . ." The motor roared and hiccupped, drowning out other sounds. The motor sounds faded. Rocinante was gone.

BLEST BE THE BOND THAT TIES

F ish bowl. Fish bowls within fish bowls.

Joe stood in the corner of a room walled with glass on two sides, feeling for all the world like a goldfish in a brandy snifter. Outside, bright sun shimmered in a courtyard lush with palm trees and oleanders. In the middle of this room sat another glass-walled room, like the hole in a doughnut. It housed bank upon bank of little red and green lights, switches, plugs and heaven knows what else in the way of electronic radio transmission paraphernalia.

Inside that room, in a still smaller glass-walled room, a pert young lady answered telephones, sometimes propping two at a time against her ears. She seemed to talk a lot, but the soundproofing took care of any hint of a voice. Joe wondered if her voice matched her cute face and shag hairstyle.

The doughnut hole contained a technician with earphones the size of cottage cheese cartons. He sat facing outward. Across from him here in this outer sanctum, two women perched on bar stools facing him. One, a bleached blond with lipstick the color of a embarrassed peach, wore earphones as big as the tech's. He was obviously talking to her as he worked his panels and switches, but only she could hear him through those phones. Joe knew the woman by name and rep—Goldie Jones, of the popular local radio talk show, "Lunch with Goldie." The other woman, looking serene and composed in a gray suit and fuchsia blouse, was Persis Magen.

From time to time on a case, radio newshounds would stick a microphone in Joe's face for a quick sound bite, and very occasionally some TV reporter cornered him for a few words; but he had never had to sit through a formal interview such as this. He couldn't imagine feeling comfortable on that hot seat, but Persis seemed to the manner born. She spoke softly, distinctly, purring into the mike without moving. Every word stood out, every phrase meant something. After twenty minutes of interview by Goldie, Persis was fielding questions called in by listeners.

Smooth as suntan lotion, Goldie slipped in with a commercial pitch for a steak house out at Cave Creek. She thanked Persis profusely, urged her listeners to go hear Persis tonight in Sun Devil Stadium, and signed off. The tech continued to do strange things inside his fishbowl, but for Persis, the business was finished.

Joe stepped forward as Persis slid off the stool.

Goldie stuck a perfectly manicured hand out at him. "Detective, drop your bio by at Suzie's desk, would you? You're terribly famous now, you know, with Brother Larry's Hour of Glory business. Besides, I'd love to do a show with a homicide cop. Inside stuff, war stories. You know."

Terribly famous. On the inside, Joe winced. On the outside, he smiled. "When I'm in the neighborhood." Joe nodded and enfolded her hand in this two.

"Pleased to have met you, Miss Jones. Persis?"

"Ready." Persis headed for the doors. Joe fell in behind, close enough to the woman that he could smell an ever-so-slight essence of perfume, understated, just like everything else about her.

The aide named Suzie came bounding out a side door to block their way. "There's a copy of the show." She pressed a cassette into Persis' hand. "Thank you so much for interviewing with us!"

"And thank you for the generous plugs. Every person who comes tonight out of curiosity has the potential to become a new soul in heaven. I appreciate you all immensely."

They exchanged a few other terms of greeting and endearment and Joe piloted Persis out into brilliant heat. They walked briskly to the station's side parking lot. Joe felt like a secret service agent, trying to watch everywhere at once. He probably looked like one too—light blue tweed sport coat and navy slacks, a tie in this weather. He popped on his sunglasses to complete the picture. Not-so-secret service.

She paused at the passenger door of their white

LeBaron. "I forget. Whose car is this?"

He unlocked the door. "My lieutentant's. We don't want to haul you around town in a patrol car, Tommy's green bug is a bit too folksy, and even if my Midget weren't out of commission, it'd be much too open." *Also, no one in your organization recognizes this car, just in case your bomber is homegrown and feels like trying again.* How savvy was this Persis Magen? She seemed so worldly wise, almost James Bondish. Did she understand things like using an unknown vehicle?

Persis slid gracefully into the seat. For such a sturdy woman, she flowed like water.

Joe settled into the driver's side. "Where next?"

Her purse gaped open in her lap as she consulted an agenda of some sort. "In fifty-three minutes I must be at 6225 North Central Avenue. How far is that do you guesstimate?"

"Valley Cathedral?"

"Yes, as a matter of fact. A prominent place?"

"Big church, with more rooms and peripheral buildings than some towns." *And plenty of places for a sniper to hide.* "We'll hop up to Bethany Home Road and over. Ten minutes. What about lunch?"

"Options?"

"Fast food, slow food, Thai, Mexican, Chinese, ribs, pizza, a vegetarian place and a spaghetti place that I can think of right off."

She folded her agenda up and stuck it back in her purse. "I heard nothing in that list to object to. Your choice. I suppose something with the menu lit up over the french fries would be most time-efficient."

Joe chuckled. "There's an ExtraBurger a block this side of Central. Their fajitas are as good as anyone's, and cola refills are free, but I hesitate to invite a nationally known celebrity to a joint like that." He gunned this monster out into traffic.

She smiled. "My kind of place." She rummaged in her purse a moment and brought out a four-page wad of notes. She glanced at Joe with twinkling eyes. "When do you plan to drop your bio by there?"

"When the cows come home."

"I thought as much." She smiled as she perused her notes. The smile faded to concentration. Motion sickness didn't seem to be one of her weaknesses.

The lieutenant's car boasted not just a phone but a fax. Modern inventions never ceased to amaze Joe. He managed to pick up the cellular and punch in Tommy's number. A cheerful Erse voice hallooed him.

"Radio interview's done and we're on our way to the ExtraBurger at Sixth and Maryland. Then Valley Cathedral."

"Extraburger! The likes of her? I'm ashamed of ye, Jose, me lad. Like taking the Queen of England to a prizefight."

"How much more incognito can she get than a fast-food place?"

"Having a fine time, I trust."

"Just peachy. Anything new?"

"Aye. I may well meet ye there."

Joe said something good-byeish and hung up. Persis had captured his attention. She scowled at the notes in her lap, twisted her face into an imitation of a California raisin, and worked her lips. Another glance, another sour face. Another. Another. She studied the next page. Same routine.

Timing is everything. She apparently came to the end of her notes just as they entered the ExtraBurger parking lot, for she jammed them back into her purse.

He licked his lips. "I can't help asking. What were you doing?"

"Memorizing. I've an address to give to hundreds of people in less than an hour, and no time to waste. A little mnemonic trick, Sergeant Rodriguez..."

"Joe."

"Joe. As I recite something to be memorized in order—in this case, the major points of my message—I let my muscles help me. The first point I recite several times as I tighten up around my right eyebrow. Second point, right cheek. Third point left cheek, fourth, left eye. If it's a two-point message I try to wiggle first my right, then my left ear. Whatever works."

"Whatever works." He hopped out and beat it around to hold the door for her. "Is that your motto? Whatever works?"

She stood up and paused a moment, thinking. "I'd say it is, yes. Whatever works." She smiled. "It's gotten me out of a variety of difficult circumstances, now that I think about it."

She led the way inside and stopped just beyond the door. A blast of air-conditioned cold hit Joe's face. She glanced about. "Order anything—fajitas are fine—whatever. I must visit the ladies' room."

"I'll wait outside the door. We're not in that big a hurry."

Her smokey eyes met his. "I am constantly impressed by your professionalism, Sergeant Rodr— Joe." And off she went in that determined way of hers.

Professionalism? Hardly. As much as she needed the ladies' room, he needed the men's room more. He abandoned his post at the restroom doors to make a quick stop himself. He popped back out into the narrow hallway moments before she emerged.

They ordered and Joe grabbed their tray—Extra-Burger was probably the fastest of the fast-food emporia. He herded her into a corner booth where, her back to the room, she was unlikely to be spotted as a celebrity and he, his front to the room, could see nearly everywhere.

She savored her fajita for only a moment before scowling. "All right, young man. What's going on with you and Marie?"

The question startled him. "Nothing."

"Exactly. I phrased it poorly. What's failing to go on between you two?"

"Mrs. Magen . . ."

"Persis."

"Persis. My partner has been trying for years to get me married off. If he hasn't been able to do it in all that time, you're not going to pull it off in a five-day try. Trust me on that. Miss Kabrhan and I relate only in a professional capacity."

"And she's been pouting and moping around ever since you interviewed her in a professional capacity last night." Persis paused to drink a heavy draft from her extraCola. "With Cat gone, Marie has had to shoulder all the duties Cat used to handle. That's why she's not with us this minute. It's not that I couldn't get temporary help in town; all manner of churches have offered highly competent personnel; but Marie needs a crush of work now to help ease her past the pain of losing her friend."

Joe thought to himself that Marie didn't seem too terribly pained, but he kept it to himself.

Persis continued, "Besides, she knows the ropes, and outsiders do not. I need her. I need her to be emotionally on top of things—as much as possible under the circumstances, of course. I need her at maximum efficiency, for she's not by nature an efficient person. If she's all upset over you, I want to correct it if possible. Vested interest, you see."

"What was the term in *Fiddler on the Roof*? Yenta. The village yenta."

Persis laughed. "Matchmaker. No. I admit you two would make a darling couple, but I advocate against a Christian becoming involved with an unbeliever. She is safe in Christ and you are not. Friendship, Sergeant Rod—Joe—is what I wish for you two. Not marriage, but not this wall of hostility I sense so vividly, either."

"You say she's not efficient by nature. Can you elaborate on that?"

Persis studied him quietly a moment and for that moment Joe feared his diversion wouldn't work. She apparently decided to let it work, for she took the bait and shifted topics. "Cat, as you know, was extremely well organized. She kept me well organized too, with no effort of my own. She kept my appointment calendar without a misstep. She made sure all obligations were met, all bills paid."

"So you said. In spite of Jules and the accounting firm."

"Ultimately the buck stops here. I *am* the organization, Joe. It's my name on the marquee. Any failure to discharge obligations falls back to me. So I keep my finger on things."

"On everything."

"Every detail."

"How many people does your organization employ?"

"A hundred and thirty in Waukesha, eleven in Canada, three each in Britain and Australia."

"Publishing arm?"

"We farm out the monthly house organ, but we're considering building our own editorial department."

Joe finished off the lettuce nest around his fajitas. "I asked you about Marie and you deftly shifted the subject to Cat, telling me what I already knew. Now let's answer the question, please."

Persis was staring at him. He raised his eyes to make sure, but he could feel her penetrating gaze without looking. She smiled suddenly, almost a smirk. "Marie. She's not a self-starter. Also, her natural gear is second, at most. She might rev up to third when she's excited. It wouldn't be noticeable if Cat and I were not both in constant overdrive. Marie gets things done, but not rapidly."

"Why keep her on the payroll if she's not productive?"

"She's productive enough. I do not expect the whole world to whip along in overdrive simply because I do. Marie is willing to do whatever must be done, and she's loyal. Those values weigh much more heavily than efficiency and raw speed."

A gaggle of noisy kids three feet high burst in through the doors. Two harried women rode herd, hazing them to the counter. It appeared either a preschool or kindergarten field trip. Three of the kids wore little plastic firemen's hats. Fire station tour. Joe thought briefly of the one time—the only time—he took his Gloria, then four, and her preschool buddies through the police station. He recalled his overwhelming urge to walk off and just leave them locked up in the holding tank, and he pitied those two young women.

They arrived at Valley Cathedral with ten minutes to spare. With just the slightest twinge of conscience, Joe parked in the only space near the doors, a handicapped slot. He could feel Persis' eyes boring into him again.

He pasted a false smile on his phiz. "I don't want you walking through the open parking lot. I can't deposit you at the door and abandon you while I go park. That leaves this. We'll both just have to live with the lie."

"Extenuating circumstances." Persis laughed heartily.

Inside a cavernous meeting hall, Persis was immediately surrounded by faithful fans. Three or four beaming, bouncing, well-groomed business types greeted her effusively and led her to a small dais on the north end. Joe positioned himself to the side of the dais and refused a dozen offers for a chair.

An older gentleman with an elegant gray moustache moved in beside him. Joe muttered, "I understand this is an invitation-only affair."

The man smiled. "More or less. Four churches in the city have an extensive evangelism program in place. Ours is one of them. We prepare men and women, lay persons, to do evangelistic work one-on-one with people, undertake short missions. It's an ambitious program, something new, and we're immensely pleased with the fruit of it. These are the graduates, so-called, from the program to date."

"Must be 400 people here."

"You've a good eye; 422 invitations. Half of them are from Valley, the rest from other churches. A special breed of godly servants, I assure you."

"Anybody from Brother Larry's Glory Assembly?"

"Glory Desert Assembly, you mean. No. they have their own program in place."

"Too bad." Joe still had not made contact with the religious radio newscaster with the big mouth. He rather wondered what the dude looked like.

He tried to get a good look at every face here, an impossible task. A few stood out, though. Maybe thirty were black, another fifteen Asian. He saw only five Hispanics easily identified as such. No Indians.

Every person here sat rapt, listening to Persis Magen, save one. Opposite side, third row back over near the side doors, a young man who looked Southeast Asian appeared unresponsive, even doleful. When everyone else laughed, he didn't crack a smile. Did he understand English? Apparently, because when Persis talked about a change in someone's life he actually scowled.

Joe nudged the fellow beside him and identified the Asian by seat and row. "He from Valley?"

"I've never seen him. Vietnamese, don't you think?"

"You know all the other church leaders in this evangelism movement, correct?"

"Yes."

"Do me an immense favor, please. Police matter. Ask around and find out which church he's from. And his name, if possible. It's important."

The mustachioed gentleman looked at Joe a long moment and Joe held his eye.

"Now?"

"Yes. Please."

"I'll see what I can do," he whispered. He moved off.

Joe watched Persis a few moments. She had, as she had mentioned, four points. Each point consisted of a funny war story, an explanation of the evangelism tactic or skill used in that situation, and the results of the Gospel in that person's life. As she launched into her fourth point, Joe saw her left eye twitch slightly. He couldn't help smiling.

Persis completed her remarks and everyone but the Asian clapped enthusiastically. The fellow with the moustache stepped up beside her, announced refreshments in another building, and promised that Mrs. Magen would field questions there. No one had mentioned to Joe that she'd be mixing with the crowd. How was he going to handle this? Or should he just pull his badge and cancel the whole show?

The people stood up and began milling toward

the doors. The Asian had disappeared. A sea of happy evangelism neophytes engulfed Persis as she moved off toward the doors firmly, purposefully. Joe tried to fight his way through the crowd to her side, but she was moving too fast and the crowd churned too chaotically. As soon as he wormed between two people, another one or two would step in front of him. They squeezed through the door and out into bright sun.

And now he lost it completely. He had no idea where she was in this ocean of heads. It dawned on him belatedly that hers was not one of those heads at all. Where could she have turned aside? And why in heaven's name should she want to?

He asked a woman beside him, "Where is the nearest ladies' room, please?"

She smiled, shrugging. "I'm sorry, I don't know. I'm from Emmanuel Press."

He darted on to the next woman. Pointing, she directed him to behind the school gym. He ran.

Here it was, labeled GIRLS. He shoved the swinging door open and yelled, "Persis! Persis?"

Nothing. He stepped inside far enough to be able to look for feet under stall doors. Empty.

Panic welled up. He was supposed to be sticking by her side, not floating around a church school yard. Where . . . ? His next best choice was to get to where she was going. He jogged out across the pavement of the side parking lot toward the reception hall.

People milled everywhere, in pairs, in clusters, talking to each other, apparently looking around in search of friends, getting in the way. Joe reached the overhang in front of the reception hall. A few dozen people had stepped inside. Not Persis.

He backtracked out across the lot. Most of the 400 filled the driveway between the main hall and the reception area now. A little white Datsun, its motor egregiously out of tune, came whiffling and popping through the crowd, headed from the far back toward the front lot. It beeped its horn impatiently, pushing itself through the main crush of the crowd, against the tide.

There she stood over by that round chapel building, underneath a tall, spreading gum tree. She gripped some woman's hands in her own as their nodding heads bobbed in unison. Joe found himself, like that Datsun, pushing his way against the tide, as the crowd poured this way and he struggled that way.

He reached Persis just as the Datsun came chugging by in first.

The Datsun's deeply tinted window rolled down two inches. In that two inches of space a glint of metal caught the sun.

Joe grabbed Persis with both arms and flung himself and her, as one, against the gum tree. His shoulder hit the unyielding tree trunk; the momentum carried Persis in a wide arc behind the tree and very nearly ripped her out of his grip. Behind them the Datsun popped and backfired.

No chance Joe could shoot back, not with all these civilians milling about. He twisted around to get a look.

The little white car revved its engine and lurched forward. Pedestrians scattered as the car hurried across the parking lot and out toward the street. No rear license plate. A sticker in the back window indicated it had been purchased recently, but Joe couldn't read the scrawled numbers. The car very nearly collided with a green Volkswagen beetle at the parking lot entrance, hung a hard, fast right, and instantly buried itself in the northbound traffic of Central Avenue.

"Joe, I do think you're overreacting. Perhaps paranoia is a better word."

He gripped her wrist and bodily hauled her off at a trot toward their car. "What's the big idea, trying to hide from me?"

"Hide from—" the lady snorted. "That's such a fatuous question I'll not dignify it with an answer."

The kelly green bug pulled alongside.

"Tommy! Baby-sit Persis here." Joe let go of the lady's wrist and sprinted to the LeBaron. In seconds he had the cellular in hand and had punched in Sammie's direct-line number. He got a BOLO out on the white Datsun instantly, but it was already too late. He knew it was too late. Too mundane a car, too much traffic, too few street cops, too many places for it to go.

His face bathed in sweat and his underarm deodorant threatening to quit, he returned to Persis and Tommy.

They herded Persis to her reception between them. Joe filled Tommy in on details as they stood on the periphery—but not too far on the periphery—watching her.

Tommy scratched his cheek. "Ye think she gave ye the slip a-purpose?"

"I really don't know. I don't even know for sure that that was a gun in the Datsun's window. Maybe metal-rimmed sunglasses. The sound could be a silencer, it could be a backfire; Conan the Barbarian tuned the engine last."

"Or untuned it to mask the sound of a silencer."

"Exactly."

"Curious. Why I stopped by, since ye asked . . ."

"Why'd you stop by here, Tom?"

"To tell ye Persis' latest plans. Originally, she was to be here a day or two after her last crusade meeting, talking with people; odds and ends at the close of the campaign. But she changed her departure date. She's taking a late-late flight out, less than an hour after her final address at the stadium."

"She didn't mention it to me."

"Nor to anyone else. Henny stumbled upon it quite by accident whilst seeking info for Harry Wallace, and called me."

Over by the refreshment table, Persis was laughing and nodding with a black man in a clerical collar. What really went on inside that graying head? Was Joe watching a callous murderer who just set up an elaborate pretense with a white Datsun in order to appear the victim? Was the Datsun happening what Joe thought it was, or was he simply too paranoid to see straight?

"Tommy, can you sit on her awhile?"

"Aye. Where are ye going?"

Joe fished out his car keys. "Judge Winteringham. Gimme your keys. You take the LeBaron."

"Jose, me lad, I smell a bond getting slapped on that lady, aye?"

"I don't want her leaving town."

"I advise against it in the strongest terms. She's got clout she hasn't even shown us yet, Jose. Item one, we'll lose any spirit of cooperation we now enjoy. Item two, your career could go somewhere in a handbasket, when she wants to continue on to Riverside for the next leg of her journey and that bond be tripping her up."

"My career's already in the handbasket, bound for Helena. Has been for two years. I'll take the flak. She's got too many question marks to let her slip away."

Tom shook his head. "No evidence strong enough, Joe."

"Motive. She mentioned today in passing, 'I *am* the organization.' You should have heard the tone of voice, the inflections. I don't have a doubt in the world that she'll do anything to protect the organization with which she identifies. Also, she boasts of keeping a finger on things. That means she surely knows everything going on, including any skulduggery."

"Not strong enough for a judge."

"The late-night ticket out should be."

"Iffy."

"Her own protection. The attempt on her life just now — she won't be protected in California, or Brazil, or wherever she's skipping out to."

"Eh, but why a bond? Surely something less drastic."

"Whatever works."

Here came the fellow in the gray moustache. The man smiled at Tom, at Joe. "I asked around, as you requested. Described the man. No one here knows your Asian fellow. He's not one of us. My secretary is going through the mailing list, trying to figure out how he might have gotten an invitation."

"Appreciate your help. Thank you." Suspicions confirmed.

"My youth pastor, Jim, mentioned one item that might be of interest. He stepped outside as Mrs. Magen finished her message. He says he saw such a man leave the hall in a hurry. Jim watched him; curiosity, I guess. He says the man went out to the back lot and got into a little white car."

VERNE'S NAMESAKE

So, *Mr.* Rodriguez. How do you like our books?"

Startled, Joe snapped forward in his chair. He pulled his feet off his desk and replaced them with the tangled pile of printouts from his lap. He stood up. "Good morning, Marie."

His first question would have been, "How did you get in here?" but one glance off toward the door and he didn't have to ask. Grace Red Morning stood there looking triumphant and then disappeared, leaving him to mollify a hurricane.

"You're despicable, do you know that?" Her face, normally so gentle, was twisted in pure malice. The hardness contrasted sharply with her soft, flowing sundress with sash. "We could have forced a court order out of you to see those records on your desk there, but Persis wanted to cooperate fully, so she gave them to you. She wants to get to the bottom of this as much as you do. And now you pull . . . that!"

"Marie, I'm sorry about that—sorry about the bond. Here, have a seat."

"I'm not staying that long. Wednesday night is our last meeting. Thursday she has to be in Riverside. Not just 'supposed to be.' Must be."

"Just a couple days ago, it was late Sunday night she had to be in Riverside. Why the change of plans?"

"Things have come up, she says."

"Frankly, I don't think we can have a suspect in custody by then. We're proceeding as quickly as we can, but you'd . . ."

Marie pressed in closer, nose to nose. "You're not listening. She *has* to be there."

"You're overestimating my legal clout. I can recommend that a person be placed under bond to prevent him from leaving the city, but I can't make it happen. That's the judge. And it's the judge who decides when it's lifted. I can't—"

"But you can recommend it."

"Riverside is California. And from there, anywhere in the world. You can't imagine the hassle involved in extradition, if any of your personnel decide not to come back to Phoenix when we need them."

"Personnel. Fine. So put *us* under bond."

"We did."

"I mean, just us. But not Persis, unless—you can't be serious. She's a suspect?"

"No one in Phoenix is above suspicion."

She rolled her eyes ceilingward and raised her

voice twenty decibels. "Oh joy! The brilliant master detective has discovered another arch criminal. You jerk! You supreme jerk! So Brother Larry's right. You really are out to destroy her work."

"For whatever it's worth, the jerk apologizes. I'm out to catch a killer, and Brother Larry's not only wrong, he's messing us up. If you really want to speed things up, get Brother Larry off our backs."

"And now you smear him too. You're more than just despicable."

Joe felt a burning need to shift this conversation away from himself to other despicable jerks. "What does your lawyer say?"

"I bet you already know. He says there's not much hope of getting it removed in time. You screwed us royally."

Joe knew this was going to happen. He had engineered the bond over Tom's objections, and now he must accept the responsibility. And he hated like deuces to hurt the gentle lady. It surprised him too how very much Marie's wrath hurt him. She was a hooker, not worth his time, let alone his emotions. And yet, all she had to do was pout and she had him by the throat. He hated himself when he didn't respond to reason.

He even stammered a bit, for crying out loud! "We're working as fast as we can. There's no vindictiveness involved, or even expediency. Necessity. It looks for the moment like Riverside is out. I'm sorry."

"I see." She stepped back slightly and her pretty little mouth formed a tight, hard line. Her voice dropped back to a decent level. "You realize it's not just a matter of life and death; it's a matter of eternal life or death for hundreds of people. No, you don't realize. And I'll bet the ranch you don't care."

He found himself saying, "I'll try to get something happening. I really will."

She glared, unsoftened. "Yeah, sure. Wish the top of the morning to your equally despicable jerk of a partner." She marched out the door. She and Grace were probably on very pleasant speaking terms. Women who think men are jerks do that.

From his desk across the aisle, Mel Carter leered. "Hang, Rodriguez, you have a way with women!"

Joe plopped into his chair and tried not to think about the knife Marie stuck in his gut with her anger. He put his feet up again and dumped the unruly heap of readouts back into his lap—Persis Magen's recent financial records. This three months' summary looked clean, every little detail. He should go through them a third time, maybe. He couldn't concentrate to save him. What he really ought to do is just dump them on Tommy.

He remembered the depths of depression that had ground him down for two years after Louise died in the crosscut canal. He thought all that was past. Now here he was right back in the pits, in the very bottom of hell again.

A tousled head flashed across his peripheral vision. Tom sprawled behind his desk across from Joe's. " 'Tis a breath of sunshine ye are, me mate."

"Top of the morning to you from Marie, equal jerk."

"She wasted no time, coming in to protest the bond."

"Yeah, and the downstairs switchboard operator says she's going to make a voodoo doll of me and start sticking in pins. Every pastor in the city's calling in to protest it. Jerry finally just put that little Gloria trick on the phone to field them all."

"Gloria? What does Jerry have against Gloria now?"

"He holds a grudge, you know that. And the Hour of Glory phone campaign is still in full swing. And the news reporters are having a real good time. Tommy, think I'll retire."

"Retire? And what be wrong with the tires ye have now?"

"Live in Cleveland and bolt bakelite handles to aluminum pots. Eight hours a day, put in my time, no decisions, go home, no hassles. I haven't seen my kids in three days."

Tom threw him a ring of keys. "Here's me car. Take the day off and go see the new orangutan exhibit. The kids'll love it."

Joe tossed them back. "If we can find some crack in this Magen thing, Persis could get to Riverside in time. I stuck her in sunny Phoenix; I should at least try to get her out."

"So take Persis Magen to the zoo. Drown her sorrows in zebracolas." Tom groped for a cigarette. "Incidentally, the quicker we put a lid on this, the happier our superior officer will be. The lieutenant's getting antsy about spending so many man-hours on surveillance this close to the end of fiscal. He called me aside this morning, impressing upon me anew the importance of frugality." He lit up in a blaze of glory; his lighter was out of adjustment.

Gretchen appeared out of nowhere to loom above Joe's right ear. "Tom, when are you gonna change brands? Can't you taste those putrid things? Wrap cowflop in a newspaper, it'd taste better." She dropped a sheaf of papers on Joe's desk. "The note you gave me last night is indeed part of a matched set."

"Cat's typewriter?"

"Yep. Same typewriter, same writer. No imagination in the phrasing. Now give me a few minutes and I'll write you a threatening note that really threatens."

"Oh, I don't know." Joe quoted from memory. " 'I hope you like Arizona because you are going to be buried here.' Not bad."

Tom waved a hand. "Sit down, voluptuous lass, and have a cigarette. Me treat."

"I'd love to, honey, but I'm on my way out. Thank heaven. Later."

Joe flapped a hand but she was already halfway to the door. He stared at Tom unseeing and Tom stared back. Joe sighed. "You didn't get anywhere with the Vacation House Motel?"

"They don't remember who made the reservations, nor who was on the desk at the time they were made. Such things are plugged into the computer by any number of employees apparently, and they don't seem all that anxious to help out a humble policeman a state away. I went so far as to phone the night clerk; woke 'im up at 9 A.M. Those bozos be cranky enough on the desk, but he was *really* hostile."

"No name resembling Jules Robinson bought airplane tickets. And they don't use credit cards, any of them. They use travelers' checks and prepaid vouchers."

Tom brightened. "Mileage on the company car! They're so swarming efficient at everything else, surely they keep close tabs on mileage. Let's call and ask."

Joe dumped the readouts and stood up. "Persis said they're happy to cooperate. Let's go a step further and look at the car itself."

"Cooperation or no, let us first collect a judge's signature on an official bit of paper." Tom stood and paused. "Probable cause?"

"Jules already lied about going through Yuma."

Tom nodded. "That's probable," and led the way out.

The team car sat parked as usual in front of Jules' room. No need to disturb Jules. Joe borrowed keys from Marie, since a stream of people were flowing in and out of Persis' kitchenette anyway. She was icy cold and very civil. He should have sent the equal jerk for the keys.

Joe slipped in behind the wheel of the company car and had to consider for a few moments why it felt wrong. The seat adjustment. The seat was a notch too far forward to be comfortable for Joe, and Jules had longer legs yet. Jules must drive like a little old lady, all hunched in a knot. What a goofus, that dude.

Tom settled into the passenger side and scooped the contents of the glove compartment into his lap. "Well now. You'll not be pinning any littering raps on them. There be three years' worth of litter here, and the car's but two years old. Gum wrappers. Little plastic lids off take-out drinks. The straw holes aren't even busted out of them."

Joe grabbed a handful out of the map pocket in the left door and started leafing through. "If you need a map of metropolitan Santa Fe, they've got it."

"Mayhap a similar chart for Riverside?"

"Nope. Phoenix, Albuquerque, Amarillo, Tulsa. Nothing from California at all."

"That signifies." Tom stuffed a wad of gum wrappers back into the glove compartment. "Saw a darlin' one-panel cartoon once. This older couple be sitting in their car, and this auto mechanic has the hood up. The engine is just covered with debris, packed solid—even a pair of gloves. And the mechanic's saying, 'I found your problem, folks—a leak in your glove compartment.' " He glanced at Joe. "Not funny, eh?"

"Better'n average."

Tom dug in his pocket. "Tell ye what, Jose. Here's me car. Take the kids and Marie and go see the orangutan exhibit."

"Will you get off the stupid orangutans? I'm okay!" Joe jammed the maps down into their pouch. He sat awhile, just staring. There is a monotony to motel doors. "Sorry, Tommy."

"No apology necessary. Everyone can use a warm body to yell at now and again. Happy to be of service."

"You're the one person in the world I shouldn't be yelling at. The apology stays." A plastic folder held the car's registration and various receipts—

tires, battery, all purchased in Wisconsin from discount outlets. From the prices he saw, Persis cut herself some wingding deals. Or maybe this was more of her travel-cheap policy, with devoted religious followers selling stuff to her at cost. Her organization's routine monthly expenses ran well over $100,000. Dollars by the dozen, but she pinched pennies until Lincoln screamed.

The vehicle had last been serviced in Albuquerque. It took Joe several minutes to copy down all the places, dates and mileages. He wrote down the current mileage. He had scant idea how far exactly was the straight-line driving distance from Albuquerque to Phoenix, but the figure was impossibly low if you subtract the distance to Riverside and back.

"Ah, now what's this?" Tom sat up from fishing about under the seat. He held a small white stub by its edges, studied it briefly and passed it to Joe. He smiled impishly, smugly.

Joe grinned for the first time all day. "Airport parking lot. You caught a live one, Tommy. Let's finish this up and talk to Jules. Officially."

From the moment he opened his motel room door, Jules assiduously ignored Joe and spoke only to Tom. Fine. When they checked in downtown, Joe sent Tom and Jules into the torture chamber together and flicked on the closed-circuit television in the next room.

The torture chamber was mostly Tom's idea, based on an article in some criminology journal. It was carefully appointed to create a quiet, pacific, restful atmosphere. Pale blue walls complemented the sienna curtains and soft pink floor lamp. The table was clear lucite, the chairs of padded naugahyde. Tom did some of his best work in the torture chamber.

As Joe watched on the monitor, Tom began by advising Jules in detail of his rights, until the man got huffy. Jules knew all that. Tom dropped rights and slipped, smooth as silk, into the next phase: profuse apology. Joe had to smile as Tom sketched the picture of a poor Irish cop just trying to do his job, shackled to a grumpy and unpredictable hot-blooded Hispanic ("perhaps yourself has noticed how edgy he is"). He apologized for having to bring Jules here in the first place. Jules bought the whole bolt.

Tom moved on to personal background, gleaning from Jules more information in five minutes than Joe had extracted in an hour at the Extraburger. The data matched what Joe had gotten: born in Naugatuck near Waterbury; attended Andover a year and dropped out; lived at home; studied inter-mittently at accounting and business, picking up a few hours here and there at various colleges.

Tom assumed a pose of liquid casualness. "Now meself is a wee bit embarrassed to have to ask this one. Why might your school record be so, ah, shall we say, so spotty?"

"This is why, right here." Jules pulled out his wallet and dug deep. From inside the "secret" flap he brought a tawny news clipping and unfolded it tenderly on the table.

Tom treated it like an antique photographic nega-tive, to be handled by the edges only. Reverently, he slid it around to where he could read it.

"Leukemia! Begorra, lad! And ye look so healthy. But then I hear that's the way with the disease. Be ye on medication now?"

"No. It's in remission. However, my days are numbered. I want to make the most of them."

"They didn't publish a picture of ye?"

"No. Just that story about how the brave little boy's fighting all the way."

"Too bad. Needs the picture. Human interest, ye see. Then the reader looks and he says, 'Ah, the pity of it. Such a fine-looking lad.' If ye were homely or ugly I could see it, but you're too attractive a fellow for ignoring. They missed a good one. What paper is this, anyway?" He flipped the clipping for clues on the back. "*Waterbury Mercury*. And here's the date on the other side here. May 18. Why almost an even three years ago. I'm delighted you're doing so chipper yet." Tom turned the clipping back over. "Stan and Mary. Nice names your parents have. Solid. Ah, and here's why they named ye Jules. They're science fiction buffs. Your middle name's Verne. Glorious! Do ye share their love of sci-fi?"

"Not really, perhaps because it's old hat to me. I was reading H.G. Wells when I was seven."

Joe had a female voice from the *Waterbury Mercury* on the other end of the line. He repeated himself. "No, May 18. Stan and Mary Robinson. I already tried information. They're unlisted. Certainly I'll wait." He watched the scene on the television monitor, but his mind was in Connecticut. Tom, bless him, was making small talk about science fiction movies, giving Joe time to write things down.

"John Whittaker." The disembodied voice of a man.

"Good morning. Joe Rodriguez, Phoenix Metro Police. We're seeking information on a Jules Robinson of Naugatuck. An article about him appeared in your paper three years ago, May 18."

"Janice just told me. Stan and Mary. I'm having her dig a little. As I recall, the stringer who gave us that story knows them personally."

"Can you tell me if a picture accompanied the article?"

"No, but I will in a minute."

"Happy to hold."

Tom was handing the clipping back to Jules. "It calls ye husky. Do they mean 'chubby?' "

"Yes. I was. The drug regimen, you know, and lack of exercise. Even for my height, chubby's putting it too kindly. I was fat then."

"You've an amazing story, lad. I've nothing but admiration for ye. For your raw courage."

Jules was lapping it up as a dog laps water.

"Mr. Rodriguez?" John Whittaker's voice was back, gruff and kindly.

"Yes sir?"

"Here's the page, and yes, there's a photo. The picture is of Jules and his parents sitting on a sofa, I suppose in their home. The father is dark, bald, spare tire. Mother has blondish hair, wearing an apron, sensible housedress, kind of dowdy. If the adults are average size, the boy's smaller than average. Dark hair, thick eyebrows like his father's. Meet in the middle; almost one big black brow. Fat. The boy's fat."

"Dark hair. Could that be a photographic quirk?"

"I don't think so. The boy looks a lot like his father and his father's dark. Swarthy. I can fax this to you."

"Would you, please? Appreciate it."

"Janice will come on the line with the parents' phone number in a minute, so don't hang up. And if you turn up some interesting little twist on this, I'd sure appreciate a tip."

"I'll remember you, Mr. Whittaker."

Tom was kiting off on a new tack. "Me partner was touching on finances—specifically betwixt yourself and Miss Dubois—when the interview at the ExtraBurger ended. I'm afraid I have to dig into that a wee bit before I let ye go. He'd have me hide if I didn't. When Miss DuBois or any of the others pay money out—here on the road, I mean—do ye record the amount immediately, or do ye accumulate slips and just enter them every now and then?"

"Everything's posted by the end of the day."

"Ah, then, ye missed one." Tom flipped the airport parking stub onto the Lucite.

"Airport?" Jules stared at it. "None of us has been to an airport. We're not flying anywhere just now, and Henry isn't in yet. Besides, that's not today's. That's . . ." Jules scowled. "That was the night after the bombing incident."

"Aye, the night someone took potshots at Miss Kabrhan and me partner."

"How did you get that? Doesn't the person who takes your money when you leave take the stub too? They do in Tulsa."

"Usually. But if the exit traffic gets so heavy it

starts backing up into the ramp, they'll wave everyone on through until the rush slows up some. Happens couple times a week. Happened that night.
Where were ye that evening? Ye remember?"

"In my room."

"The company car wasn't out front."

"The spaces were all taken. I had to park way off,
near those bushes with the white flowers."

"Ah. Oleanders, they are. Lovely this time of year,
eh?"

"Hello?" An older male voice on the phone
grabbed Joe's attention.

"Hello, Mr. Stanley Robinson? My name is Sergeant Joe Rodriguez, Phoenix, Arizona, Police.
We're engaged in an investigation here that in-
volves your son Jules. I wonder if you ..."

"Police? What is this, some kind of sick joke? You
sick or something? You know what the penalty is
for impersonating a policeman, pal?"

"No joke, Mr. Robinson. If you doubt me, I'll
hang up and let you call the department yourself.
Area code 602. Ask information for our number. My
extension here is 4483."

"Arizona! What could possibly be out there that
includes Jules?"

"Frankly, sir, it's a murder investigation concern-
ing the evangelistic team with whom your son is
associated. We traced you from a clipping he car-
ries in his wallet and we ..."

"My son wasn't never associated with no evangelistic team. He took some accounting courses. He
was gonna be an accountant, maybe work in a cancer hospital or research place. No religious stuff.

He wanted to help by saving them money. As good as making money, y'know, saving money. He had a good head for figures."

"Mr. Robinson, you're referring to your son in the past tense."

"Of course I am. Jules died of leukemia two years ago."

ZOO NEWS

On the periphery of her mind, Marie noticed a van pull up in the end parking slot because the front parking spaces were full. A screen of oleanders blocked out just about everything except the rumble of its monstrous motor.

She had always wanted to sit in the shade of a palm tree. Here in Phoenix she was fulfilling that dream. Palm trees don't afford nearly as much shade as you might expect. Her iced tea was almost gone. So was her afternoon break. In a few minutes she'd have to leave this motel patio, with its flowers and trees — this palm, a lacy little tree with lime green bark, a couple bushlike trees with long, narrow leaves — and return to the nondream world of paperwork and appointments.

Then she heard the voices. Tom and Joe. Her breastbone did a little tickle, as if she were a high school girl watching a TV heartthrob. Stupid!

She watched the van, bits and pieces through the hedge. Joe swung the driver's side door open, but he didn't get out. "Tommy, you do it, all right? It's your thing, not mine."

And Tom Flaherty's brogue purred, "Will ye trust me instincts on this? She'll open up better if you're around. Now you're gonna have to give her the impression that everything's peaches and cream. Professional relationship."

"She was jerking us off with that purity scam, Tommy. Don't you realize what kind of girl she is?"

"Was, Joe. Was. No evidence that she's plying her former trade. Ye got to put it aside. I need ye on this."

"All right. Let's get it over with."

"That's not the attitude ye should be engendering. Let's be positive. Expectant."

"I look forward to getting this over with. Better?"

"Hardly." Tom swung out of the van and strode away toward the motel room door.

Now what should Marie do? *When all else fails, be honest,* Persis often said tongue in cheek. Marie would have to settle for semihonest. Casually, she stood up and turned so that Joe would see her, or at least notice her movement behind the hedge. She picked up her magazine and the remains of her iced tea and headed for the motel room.

She stopped and put some effort into looking properly surprised—not too much and not too little—as Joe slid out from behind the van's wheel. It was an extremely dusty, boxlike vehicle.

"Marie."

"Joe." She smiled, and tried to keep the smile from looking like she meant it. She found his rugged looks very attractive; not exactly handsome in the classic Paul Newman sense, but those eyes. . . .

Joe grimaced and pretended it was a smile. He whistled toward Tom. The Irishman had stepped inside the motel. He reappeared and came bounding back. Joe nodded toward the van. "We're going over to Tempe and pick up my two kids for the afternoon. Their cousins are gone for a couple days, so they're at loose ends. Tommy thought you might like to come along." He was wearing jeans and a blue chambray shirt, its sleeves rolled halfway to his elbows. He looked very outdoorish. Tom was in a striped cowboy shirt Garth Brooks would have envied, but he still looked like a city man. Curious, the difference.

"Oh sure. Yes, it sounds nice. But Persis . . ."

"Meself has already cleared it with her." Tom grinned.

Marie bobbed her head and asked no more questions. "Let's go."

Cousins. That would be the sister's three that Tom mentioned. She let Tom escort her to the passenger side and hold the door for her. She crawled up into the seat and struggled with her seatbelt. "Do you two always double-date like this?"

"Eh now, Marie, this be no date. 'Tis business. In-depth interview." Tom pulled his cigarette pack, studied it a long moment and put it away. He closed her door and bolted up into the seat behind her. He slammed the side door.

"At least you're honest about it. Or it's a super

line." She finally got her seatbelt snapped. "I understand, gentlemen, that this is supposed to be a business meeting. Let's get down to business." She had no idea where they were headed, but Joe drove with the casual air of a man who knew every corner of the city. And he probably did.

"Ebenezer Scrooge ye are. Very well. First, about Jules. Can ye remember him ever using another name? Going by another name?"

"An alias?" She frowned.

"Aye."

"No."

"Think about it awhile. An old driver's license? Insurance membership? Letter from home? Some little joke he pulled and used another name to cover?"

"Oh, he pulled a million jokes, none of them funny. But I can't remember that he ever used an alias."

"Ye mentioned he does weird things. For instance?"

"Well, actually, not lately. His boasting is mostly about what he did earlier. Like I say, he's changed immensely in the last couple years."

"All right. An incident from the past he's boasted of."

"When he was young he'd catch tomcats and tie their tails together; a knot he called sizing or something."

"Seizing?"

"That's it. Some little old lady caught him once. I guess it was her cat. Cops picked him up for a couple different stunts like that. They didn't really do anything, although to hear him tell it he barely escaped the chair. Another time he made this little neighbor girl—" She stopped. "That was really sick. I guess the kid wasn't twelve yet. They almost nailed him on that one but the girl's mother got scared and squelched it. Hushed it up. They had money, I think."

"All this where he was growing up?"

"Apparently. But I don't think it was Andover." The air conditioning in this van was certainly nothing to write songs about. Even though the fan howled, Marie was pouring sweat. And the unit put out a strange musty odor.

Joe seemed not the least bothered by the heat. "Marie, the night someone tried to blow us off Camelback Mountain, Persis slipped out for a walk alone. Our people lost track of her for about four hours. Did she ever give any indication to you where she went?"

"Oh, she does that. She walks alone a lot in Waukesha. Helps her think. When she gets a mental block she walks it out. How did she manage that?"

"After Tommy left she went out with Harry, ostensibly to stop at a minimart. While Harry was picking up some snack stuff, she slipped out the back. Seems very practiced at dodging. He saw she was gone within seconds and she had already disappeared."

Marie giggled. "Bet that's not the only time, either."

"Twice since then. And I lost her yesterday at Valley Cathedral."

"If I know her, it's become something of a

game—giving your professional spies the slip, sneaking off to be alone."

Joe snarled, "She's going to end up in protective custody if she keeps playing her little game."

"Haven't you bugged her bad enough? What are you trying to prove, anyway?"

"Who killed Cat DuBois."

"Children! Children!" Tom waved his hands. "Let us not curdle the milk of human kindness with the gastric juices of hostility. Marie, do ye know if Jules ever actually did time for any of his shenanigans?"

"Often in hot water but never boiled, that I know of."

"Does he hold grudges?" Joe turned right onto a broad, nearly empty street through virtually undeveloped desert. The boulevard curved up through a rocky saddle and she wondered if this were the economy-sized lover's lane he mentioned that night (it seemed so long ago).

She replied, "Pouts a lot. Refuses to talk to you for days, occasionally weeks. Sooner if he wants a favor. But then he seems to dismiss it."

"Does he get mad at some people more than others?" Tom asked.

"Always at those he considers below his rank; never at those he considers above him."

"Frequently toward you and Cat, never toward Persis?"

"Right." She watched for a few quiet moments the wonderful array of flowers splayed out along both sides of the road. "Are these flowers wild or planted?"

"Wild," Joe replied. "We had good winter rains

this year. Desert annuals need winter rain to sprout."

"Do you know their names?"

And Joe Rodriguez seemed to soften, to loosen up. He waved a hand in general toward the drifts of yellow flowers that nodded along the road berm and crept in broad, open patches across the bare desert soil. "Poppies. The leggy salmon-colored flowers by those rocks there are desert mallow, Sphaeralcea. The purple spikes over there—and there—are lupines." He named a few more, and then they turned left at a light and crossed a very old cement bridge over a dry riverbed.

They had mentioned Tempe. This must be it. She rode in silence as they wound back into the older part of town along residential streets. Joe pulled up beside a big, square, two-story house. He got out and walked inside.

Was this the time to ask? She was dying of curiosity, and now seemed as good as not. "I didn't notice until Persis mentioned it, but Joe doesn't have any grip in his right hand. He makes a cup shape with it, like when he's shifting gears, but not a grip. And his right leg acts funny sometimes." She turned to Tom. "I bet there's a story there."

"Two years ago, a gentleman offed his girlfriend in a fit of pique." Tom's expressive face tightened a little. "We were apprehending the perp out on one of Joe's turfs, the South Mountain Speedway. Joe thought of being a professional driver once, y'know, when he was young and foolish."

She remembered the headlong, careening chase down that winding road on Camelback. "Still drives like it sometimes."

"Aye! We were closing on the fellow, a stock-car driver. That is, approaching him. He must have seen the backup—that would be your uniformed cops—blocking the exits. He hopped in his car, aimed it at what he thought was the only way out, and then veered off toward a different hole at the last moment—a hole Joe and meself happened to be blocking. He ran over Joe. Right over him. Joe spent about a year getting the use of his right side back. He qualifies every quarter on the firing range, so he's back in the saddle again."

"Did you catch the driver?" She was watching the front porch for Joe's return. The silence made her turn to look at Tom. "Tom?"

"Aye." He barely breathed the word. She studied his face, trying to see meaning there. The silence must have weighed too heavily, for he completed the thought. "Twas the only time I ever fired me weapon in the line of duty."

The back door of the van clunked open and Joe plopped a big picnic basket inside it. He came around and climbed back into the driver's seat.

He pointed. "There they come."

A boy and a girl came running down the street. They hurried directly into the house with their bookbags. Moments later they popped back out. The boy paused to lock the front door. Breathlessly they clambered in the side door of the van and settled into their seats. Obviously they'd done this many times. Tom reached out with his long arm and hauled the side door shut.

Joe started the motor and pulled the van out into

the street. "Rico there is nine and Gloria is six. Call her Glo. This is Miss Kabrhan, a friend."

For the next five minutes Marie made small talk with small people and was impressed with their sophistication, and with an intriguing mix of shyness and eagerness. They obviously viewed her as a possible mother. Questions like, "Do you like to cook, Miss Kabrhan?" and, "Are you married, Miss Kabrhan?" and, "Do you like kids, Miss Kabrhan?" provided her first clues. They were polite, though. She could tell that Joe was a strict disciplinarian even though he didn't correct them here. She envied these children. Her own father's discipline had been so erratic, either unduly harsh or altogether absent.

They were following signs to the zoo and botanical garden. Joe turned aside and parked in the zoo lot. Instantly the children bolted out of the van. Rico held the passenger door open. Tom climbed out and headed to the back for the picnic basket. Marie slid out. This van stood unusually high off the ground.

She smiled at Rico as he closed the door. "Thank you."

He grinned and shrugged. "Anytime. Hey, if I quick hold the door, I don't get stuck carrying the basket."

From behind Marie, Joe said, "That's what you think, pal." The picnic basket sat at his feet and he had scooped little Glo up. She perched on his left arm with her legs straddling his side.

They crossed a broad, brick-paved bridge over a moat, from parking area to entrance kiosk. Rico lugged the basket and Joe carried Glo, not because she needed carrying but so they could converse nose to nose.

All the way across, Glo babbled about the terrible, horrible things that had happened to her in school that day. One little arm clung to his shoulder and neck; the other flapped about in eloquent gesture. Joe nodded sagely. Marie listened for him to take sides with or against her teacher. He carefully did neither. He nodded and empathized and asked questions. The little girl absolutely basked in her daddy's attention.

How many years did Marie yearn for a daddy's attention. She still did. Her heart ached anew.

The blue-haired lady in the kiosk greeted Joe and Tom by name and cast a closely analytical eye at Marie whom she obviously considered to be Joe's date. If she only knew that he despised Marie. . . . He gave the woman a guest pass for Marie and they walked inside, from the dark of the roofed entranceway into afternoon brilliance.

Marie had visited a zoo only once in her life, and that was a grade school field trip. She expected a solemn cluster of cages with listless animals peering out. The first thing to catch her eye was the gift shop by the entrance, all chrome and glass and inviting. They strolled up over a rise, with trees and dense shade to their left and bright, broiling sun to the right. The whole place felt airy, open, cheerful, spacious. She loved it already.

They settled in cool shade beneath tall, dark trees near the children's zoo. The kids swirled about like a hurricane, with Joe and Marie at the eye.

"I like this zoo—it's not what I expected at all."
Marie turned to face Joe. "You really appreciate
plants and animals and nature, don't you."

Tom was setting out paper plates and flatware.
"Now and again, ye know, he takes tours out into
the desert. Safaris. 'Tis why the Suburban be so
dusty." He unpacked the picnic basket, peeking ap-
preciatively inside each Tupperware container he
lifted out. "Ah! Potato salad! His gimmick is that
he's quarter Yaqui, so his clients get an Indian's
perspective on the forbidding wasteland, ye might
say." He stood erect. "There ye go, Jose! Take Marie
out for a tour."

Marie didn't think but a moment about the intriguing prospect of really seeing the desert she had
been driving through since Oklahoma. "I'd love it."

Joe smiled noncommittally. "We'll have to discuss it. Back in Waukesha, does Jules have his own
office space?"

So. It was back to business, the Scrooge. "No. He
only handles work when we're on the road."

"You work out of Persis' office?" Joe was building a row of sandwiches. He had laid out five slices
of bread. Now he was dealing cheese slices onto
them.

"Yes."

"And in his dealings with you, Persis, or Cat,
Jules would come to Persis' office or go to Cat's?"
He twisted the lid off a mayo jar as Tom opened a
container of lunchmeat.

Marie shook her head. "Cat didn't have a separate office. We're all together."

Joe stopped, the mayo knife poised midway. It

blurted out of him unguarded. "But one of the major budget items is separate office space for Cat."

Marie looked at him, frowned, opened her mouth, then closed it again. How ought she respond? Her mind was spinning, absolutely spinning. She must handle this just right. If he knew too much, or not enough, everything was lost. Destroyed. She wouldn't get a second shot at it, either.

Joe glanced at Tom. Tom raised his eyebrows and pressed his lips together.

Rico came slamming up against the table. "I'm going over to the orangutans, okay? I'll be right back."

"Where's Glo?" Joe started spreading mayo on the top slices.

"Right there." Rico swung an arm in about three directions.

Joe nodded grimly. The boy raced off.

Marie accepted the sandwich and apple offered her, but she didn't eat. She lowered her head and closed her eyes. The blessing on her food she mentioned to God quickly. The bulk of her prayer was a request for a quick wit. This was a perilous moment. How much did Joe really know? Was he bluffing? Guessing?

Her heart was thumping so loudly they surely must be able to hear it. *The Telltale Heart*. Poe. Same thing. She bit into her sandwich and chewed a moment. "I can see, gentlemen, that I'm a failure at being a murderer just as I'm a failure at everything else. Those entries in the books for Cat's office—they were payments to me, to keep me quiet. The accounting firm was none the wiser. Cat never looked at the books. Then one day she called the spread sheet up on her screen and saw it. She started to make trouble."

"You're saying," said Tom, "that Persis not only took part in blackmail, but is a murder accomplice. Right?"

"Wrong. I deliberately picked a sum that wasn't too extravagant, just so she'd go along with it without kicking. She didn't like it, of course, but she figured paying me was better than ruining her reputation. The things I threatened to spill would have hurt her operation badly and she knew it. But she had nothing to do with Cat's death. That was strictly my idea."

"And the bomb that night?" Joe's voice was tight.

"I thought my timing was pretty nice. She always takes a shower when she gets back. You almost broke my ribs, though, you clod. Couldn't you have moved behind the cabinet a little more?"

"Where'd ye get the bomb, lass? And the bomber?" Tom, the perpetual eater, had laid his sandwich aside.

"Peter's friend. Peter was my pimp; you dug that out already. He has this friend here in Phoenix. They served in Nam together. Demolitions. That's why I chose Phoenix, was for Pete's friend. He wired the car bomb and threw the satchel both."

"And the purpose of the second bomb, lass?"

"So no one would guess that Cat was supposed to be the victim. I think now that it might have been a mistake. I should have left things the way they were."

"Exactly how much is the sum set aside for Cat's

office, so to speak?"

"You've got all you're going to get, Irish. From now on I talk with a lawyer present, all legal-like."

Glo arrived breathless from the play area, still babbling, and stood on her knees on the picnic table seat beside her daddy. Joe popped open a pocket knife and cut her sandwich into quarters. She grabbed a quarter and some grapes and ran back to her seat on the little merry-go-round.

Joe waited until she left. 'Why are you spilling this now? Why confess at all?"

Marie shrugged. "I don't know. It just came out. I think for one thing I'm kind of proud of it. The timing. The setup. Clever, don't you think—even if it didn't have any hope of working? And I wanted to make sure somebody else sees how clever I am. And guilt. Half of Persis' religion rubbed off on me. The guilt part. The load was getting too heavy. And if you arrested Jules for it, or Persis, or even some stranger, I'd *really* have a load. I'd have to confess anyway. I couldn't take that. Somebody else getting the blame and the credit—y'know?

Joe rubbed his cheeks and sighed. "So why did you send someone out that night to put bullets through my windshield? More red herrings?"

"That's strictly your problem. I had nothing to do with that. I was scared out of my skull." She popped some grapes into her mouth. "Dessert and the police station in that order, right? You can't imagine how much better I feel now." She flourished her sandwich. "Bon appetit, gentlemen."

They had cleared another case, a biggie, and Joe

felt so wretched he could puke. It was over. Anticlimactic. A logical suspect confesses, the confession rings true, the reason for confessing smacks of authenticity. It was all over except for the confirming evidence, and probably it would be Joe who assembled it.

Everything fit. Her voice rang false when she spilled her confession, but you could attribute that to nervousness beneath a casual exterior. Joe realized now how hard he had been wishing it were Jules. That's life. Pits!

He cradled the phone receiver as Tom came ambling in.

"Top of the morning, Jose. Sleep well?" He sprawled out across Joe's desk and propped his head in one hand.

"No, and neither did you. What're you doing in the office this early?" Joe stretched out his legs and leaned back.

"Call the judge yet about lifting Persis' bond?"

"Just now. Caught him shaving. He'll take care of it." Joe shoved a piece of paper across his desk.

Tom picked it up. "Richard Lee Spesch. Who might that be?" He brightened. "Jules Robinson! How did ye ever find him?"

"Since the fingerprint angle didn't net us anything, I did a little elementary detecting on the phone. If he was half the nut Marie paints him to be, he'd have quite a reputation around his high school, and if he read the *Waterbury Mercury*, he likely lived somewhere within, say, a fifty-mile radius. So I called high school principals in the area."

"A graduate of four or five years ago?"

Joe nodded. "He graduated a year late because in his junior year he was suspended five months. His principal remembers him well. He faxed us school pictures and other records for confirmation."

"Delightful fellow, that. Assumes the identity of a boy he reads about in the paper, since his own past be checkered. No wonder I found nothing on him. The real Jules was straight. Fiendishly clever. Why couldn't we get a read on prints?"

"His juvenile records are locked up; we need a court order to learn anything about him prior to age eighteen. I don't know how he managed to swing that. Apparently, though, he kept himself out of official trouble after eighteen."

Tom abandoned the desk in favor of the chair. He thunked his feet up. "Do me a favor. Let Jules/Richard think he has us fooled. This little tidbit will be a dandy shocker, should I need it sometime."

"Sure." Joe lapsed into contemplation of the tops of his boots.

Tom clapped his hands. "Jose, me lad, I feel good again. I didn't think that cute little number could be a bomber. Although it's still possible she is, I aver."

"Not possible. Probable. The only real kink in her tale is that airport parking stub. If she can give us enough inside facts—approximate dates, amounts of payoffs, things like that—she's it."

Tom nodded. His eyes widened suddenly. "Begorra! Did ye leave word at the jail?"

"I thought 'begorra' was an Irish stereotype and beneath your dignity. What word?"

"Visitors! Persis or Jules to give Marie the facts and figures she needs to make her story complete.

Persis has to get to Riverside, aye? If there be a suspect in the cage, Persis squirms out from under bond in time to make her meetings and such. So Marie throws herself to the wolves and good-bye Persis." Tom dived for the phone.

Joe's breastbone went thump. "Then Marie has two choices: take the rap if she thinks Persis did it and she's loyal, or change her plea and deny everything once Persis is on the road again. And I fell for it! Hang it, Tommy, I fell for it!"

How did Persis say it? *Marie is willing to do whatever must be done, and she's loyal.*

Tom grunted into the receiver. "Izzat so? Aye, Maude, if ye would. There's a grand lass. Mmm... mmm." He scowled at Joe. He scowled at the receiver too, before he cradled it. "They beat us to it. Persis and her lawyer were in half an hour ago. They talked heads together for a good twenty minutes. Maude's closing the barn door for us now that the horse's been stolen."

Joe looked around for something to throw. Nothing appeared heavy enough to vent his anger. "Whatever information Marie needed to provide a convincing story she has now. No, Tommy. Surely she wouldn't sell herself on a murder rap unless she actually did it. Persis wouldn't let her. If Persis has any sense of human decency at all..." His voice trailed off.

Of course Persis would let her. The two women shared a common goal—the saving of sinners by Persis' preaching. Marie would make any sacrifice to serve that goal. See how Persis praised her loyalty? And what if Persis were the killer? She was a powerful and influential woman, well able to duck legal problems. Nothing short of a lengthy extradition fight would bring her back to Phoenix if she were serious about staying away. The world, already gray, turned black. Now what?

Tom looked no cheerier. "Joe? That factory in Cleveland where you're gonna retire and bolt handles to saucepans—would ye think they might have two openings?"

THE MOP-UP MAN

The mess surrounding that Louie the Hype case was beginning to clear a little. They might even get Louie a nice long set of consecutive sentences. The Persis Magen thing was neatly sewed up, at least in theory. News of Marie's arrest even stanched the flow of protesting phone calls from all those Hour of Glory listeners.

Three different newspaper reporters that Joe knew of were poking around trying to find some little morsel that would suggest Marie had been set up to take the fall by her powerful employer. A *Republic* editorial had already suggested it.

The religious nuts on one side and the antireligious nuts on the other. Joe absolutely abhorred this case.

The only other active case in his hopper was the Ringgardner business, and he couldn't do any more with that until next month. Joe felt at loose ends. Betrayed, even, although why he felt betrayed he could not imagine. He slammed the lap drawer in his desk and tried to convince his body it ought to stand up. His right leg was stiff. Maybe a weather front was coming in.

He reached for the phone without really thinking and poked out the lab extension numbers.

A grating tenor answered. Fortunately the lady looked much more feminine in person than her harsh voice suggested.

"Joe Rodriguez, Mrs. Ruskin. Gretchen there?"

"Just a minute." Their hold button put a buzz in the line.

Gretchen's cheerful voice, "Good morning, Joe. I'm open to marriage proposals. Biological clock, y'know. What can I do for you?"

"Marriage, no. Interesting courtship, maybe. You made a casual remark a day or two ago—'I'll write you a note that really threatens.' Remember?"

"I remember you liked the existing ones just fine."

"Changed my mind. You studied those notes. Did you . . ."

"Memorized the bloody things."

"How do you pigeonhole the writer?"

"You're asking for a psychological profile based on some crank notes?"

"Why not? Women can do anything men can do, you said. Freud wouldn't have hesitated."

Gretchen blew a raspberry. "Immature. He doesn't know much about life. His idea of a dirty movie is a 1955 Brigitte Bardot flick. Confused. Ambivalent. He wants to lash out and hurt, and yet he's afraid to."

"You keep saying 'he.' "

"You don't think a woman would write that swill, do you?"

"Wouldn't dream of it. That masculine, huh?"

"And immature."

"Right. Unacquainted with life. Gretch? Suppose a mature, worldly-wise woman wrote the notes that way deliberately, just to cast suspicion on some poor, defenseless little immature male. Possible?"

"You think of the weirdest things. Yeah, it's possible. But now you're talking about a psychiatrist turned bomber. Or at the very least a degree and experience in psychology."

"Persis Magen holds an earned doctorate in psychology."

"However, she's too open and spontaneous. Oh, she plans her work and all. But she's too volatile. She's not a drawn-out premeditator."

"Marie Kabrhan handles a lot of counseling chores."

"Too innocent. She'd never . . ."

"Like blazes she is. Her rap sheet starts at fifteen and goes downhill from there."

"No, Joe, I mean it. Innocent. Her attitude toward life, toward people, toward her work. No matter how many mistakes she made, no matter what she's been through, she's sweet and caring. Bet she's a darned good counselor too, if that's what she does. Especially if she was a hooker once. She's been there."

"But she . . ."

"Hang it, Joe, you asked for a profile. I'm giving

you one. Not Marie."

"That leaves Jules and Barbrie."

"Who's Barbrie?"

"He just flew in yesterday evening. Jules is their advance man and he's their rearguard. If you think Jules is backward, wait'll you meet Henry. Shy as a woodland violet except when he's talking religion. Mousy little guy about five-four. Tries to look grown up by keeping his moustache long."

Gretchen clucked into the phone. "How does Persis manage to latch onto such loonies?"

"No doubt the same way Maynard Rust does. Thanks, Gretch. I appreciate your help." He cradled the receiver, silencing her string of expletives.

Gretchen's analysis of the notes agreed with his. But she had a double major in psychology and forensic chemistry to back her up, and Joe was only a mild-mannered Associate of Arts graduate of a great metropolitan junior college. He liked the corroboration. Professional.

Marie. Who would've guessed?

He yanked off his clip-on tie and opened his collar button, unplugged the jack from his phone, put up his feet and sat back. It was his message to the world—more specifically to the girls in the office—that he was not to be disturbed. He arranged facts and surmises into categories, a sort of chronological master picture. There were holes. He wrote himself notes about holes to be plugged, data to be filled in.

He ruminated first on Marie's role in the business. Gretchen called her sweet and innocent. That showed how much Gretchen knew. On the other hand, his first impression of Marie had been exactly that. Sweet and innocent and caring. Marie called herself clean. Persis had talked about the washing of the lifeblood of Jesus, cleansing the stains of sin. Joe had heard those words his whole life — at least, that part of his life when he was still being sent to church.

Persis had talked about the old and new natures of the believer. Was innocence Marie's new nature? If so, how strongly did the old nature, the old familiarity with crime and filth, intrude itself? Nobody can erase the effects of years of prostitution. Marie.

Then his cerebral flight stalled out. He tried to concentrate on Jules, but his mind kept skipping back to Marie. He attempted to sift the contradictory evidence touching Persis. She would soon be in Riverside, thanks to Marie's confession. Marie. No doubt this was another of those answers to prayer that Persis took so much for granted. Pray to go to Riverside and your henchman — henchgirl — will make it come true. Marie.

Persis claimed that God honors those who do His will. Obviously she considered herself a member of that group. How could she be doing His will if she was involved in bribery, blackmail and probably murder? And if she were so tainted, why did God so cheerily and promptly grant her requests? Marie.

How about this milktoast Barbrie? Tom was with him now in the torture chamber. Barbrie's life seemed even more lacklustre than Jules' — the real Jules, not this Spesch. His personality was as exciting as a furniture commercial, his lifestyle as colorful as canned pears. Marie.

Girls with a past have such appealing skills to bring into a relationship. What if she really were cleansed of her filth and guilt? She would be a pure woman, essentially, and yet experienced, a pro who knew how to please a man. An intriguing mix. Marie. It took Joe long minutes to realize where his fancy was taking him. His neck flushed, not in embarrassment, but in anger with himself. Crime and debauchery can be paid for, to a point. They cannot so casually be erased. Even a twenty-year sentence at Florence can't obliterate crime and sin completely.

Joe fidgeted with the pencils on his desk. Marie Kabrhan. Such a cute girl. Sweet-looking. A baby and years of experience, and here she sat pretending she was religious. If Joe ever considered marrying again, it would be to a fat, homely girl with warts. Then he could be reasonably assured she was wholesome if she said she was. There was a limit to his admiration of professionalism, and Marie went way beyond it.

He glanced over at the plain and pallid wall clock—9:45. He had been sitting here over an hour with nothing at all to show for it. Disgusted by all his mental short circuits, he straightened his tie and plugged the phone back in. He was halfway out of his chair when it rang. He answered.

"*Miss* Wiemer here. The Honorable Miz Wiemer as far as you're concerned, you jerk. Pick my brain and then insult me. Two things didn't show up in the lab report on those notes. Maynard didn't agree with me. He says we should stick to facts and demonstrable surmise and this is conjecture. Flimsy."

"I apologize profusely, Lord High Gretchen. May

you be our next district attorney by a landslide margin. I value your judgment; you know that. Also your conjectures. What do you have for me?"

"I may or may not take your apology under advisement. One is that I think the guy who typed those notes is left-handed. Also—"

"From the relative pressure on right and left letters?"

"No. Electric typewriters take care of all that. Also, I think he took a high school typing course and has had very little typing experience since then."

"Now how do you get all that?"

"There were four errors, remember? Strikeovers." Her voice sounded pleased, even smug. "The particular errors he made were all on a long reach of the right index finger. His hands were in the proper position probably, but the finger wasn't making it. Inaccurate. Not accustomed to stretching out there to nail the right key."

"Probably not computer literate."

"Probably not. Right. All this is just my personal guess, understand. Don't lay it at Maynard's door or he'll fry me." Gretchen's voice paused. "Joe? You still there?"

"Sorry. Thinking. Persis and Jules are both left-handed. Don't know about Barbrie. Hey. In his first interview, Barbrie told Tom he has trouble with coordination. Not just fine control but gross coordination. Major movements. No finesse. Could your strikeovers be due to lack of coordination rather than lack of practice?"

"Could. But then all his fingers should be uncoordinated, not just one of them."

"Mmmm. Gretch, I appreciate your ideas on this, more than you realize. Thanks for taking the trouble."

"That's the nicest thing you've said to me in years. There's hope for you yet, Rodriguez."

"Crack the case for us and I'll consider paying you another compliment maybe. Sometime."

"Deal. I'll do anything for adulation. Later."

"Later."

The line blanked out, empty. He hung up. So Maynard considered that to be shaky conjecture. Joe must be careful not to let Gretchen's hunches weigh too heavily. On the other hand . . .

He headed for the elevators.

Joe entered the barren little room beside the torture chamber. Harley and Turk were sprawled out on folding chairs, staring at the TV monitor. Joe leaned on the wall behind them and watched the screen from over Turk's head.

The TV eye was watching the room next door, as Tom sat across from Henry Barbrie. He had Henry spinning like a gyroscope, explaining the wonderful interworking of Persis and the Holy Spirit.

Harley jotted another scrawling line across his notebook. "That Irishman is the Larry Bird of investigators. Babe Ruth. He's amazing."

"Muffle it," Turk hissed. "I can't hear."

Tom leaned his elbow on the Lucite tabletop and cupped his cheek in his hand, presumably enraptured by Henry's discourse. "That's not an ounce short of marvelous. Would ye go so far as to say, then, that Persis can commit no error?"

Henry laughed. "Absolutely not! Any servant can fail. Paul said that over and over in his epistles. Look at David, Tom. He sinned grievously with Bathsheba, and paid for it his whole life. He fell from grace in the matter of bringing the ark home, despite his good intentions. And the census. And yet he was the apple of God's eye. 'For the sake of My servant David.' Over and over."

"David. King David, ye mean? I'm not too familiar in that area."

"It's no sin to be ignorant of God's Word, Tom, but it's error to continue in ignorance. The story of David and Bathsheba is in 2 Samuel, uh, 11, I believe. I think bringing the ark up is 2 Samuel 6. Six or 7. Or 5 is it?"

"And so Persis does make mistakes now and again."

"Of course. We all do. We'll not achieve perfection this side of the veil. But David offered full and genuine repentance. Remorse and repentance. And even in his deepest despair, he praised the name of the Lord. Read his Psalm 13. And 22. And 38. He lived fully for God even when he erred. And Persis is like that too."

"Then it can't be mattering much what ye do so long as ye repent properly afterward. Especially since we're bound to make mistakes anyway."

Henry hardened in his insipid way. "I didn't say that. You're making fun of God's provision for—"

"Not at all, I assure ye!" Had Tom a forelock, he surely would have tugged it. "I meant no offense. I'm serious. So long as ye seek forgiveness and express your repentance, ye should be able to get away with murder. Ye told me not three minutes ago that God can forgive all—even murder."

Henry sighed. "Let me start over. When Adam sinned in Eden . . ."

"Wish he'd get off all that religion jazz," Turk grumbled.

"Don'tcha see where he's going?" Harley grinned. "This Barbrie spouts Magen's line. If Persis Magen thinks she can cop out and repent—you know, beat a murder rap before God's judgment seat—she just might try it. Or one of her underlings. Especially if she offs somebody to preserve God's good name. Joe was talking about them maybe protecting the organization's rep."

Joe chimed in. "That religion jazz is the whole crux of the case, maybe. Everyone concerned takes it far too seriously for us to soft-pedal it."

Henry was rolling along under a full head of steam now. "The Old Testament sacrifices as outlined in Leviticus, first seven chapters, dealt only with unintentional sin. Intentional sins had to be corrected—rectified—reversed—before they could be atoned for. These sacrifices are a type, or shadow, of the supreme sacrifice that was to come, Jesus Christ Himself. He made full restitution once for all. Now. When you accept that fact—that is, accept that Jesus paid the full penalty for your sin, all that you've done in the past is paid for. Erased. Blotted out. Gone. You're pure again. A fresh start. *But* from that point forward you must . . ."

Marie. Her name lit up like neon in Joe's mind. Marie purified. She had said so. Persis said so. Barbrie was saying so.

Marie constantly intruded, kept inserting herself into Joe's thoughts, and he hated himself because of it. Surely he could control his own mental processes better than this! He thought about the fury and consternation on her face when she exploded in the office. The pain stabbed anew.

"... sinning with the idea of erasing it all later with a few glib words, I assure you—it will not erase so easily. I refer you to Hebrews 10."

"So ye wouldn't think Persis could do anything rash?"

Henry's eyes went wide. "Like kill Cat, you mean? Unthinkable!" He launched into another Scripture-laden discourse on accountability.

One of Joe's questions to Persis would have been, "Why did you hire these two men, Jules and Henry, over others that might be interested in your work?" He saw now that, however deficient Henry seemed in some ways, he knew his Bible inside out. He knew the tenets word on word, line by line. Apparently one of his tasks was to establish Bible studies for new believers converted at the meetings. For that he would be excellent. Not only must he know about every study ever devised, but he himself was living proof of the fruit of study. And, as Marie had mentioned, he was not in any way threatening.

Tom had come about on a fresh tack. "Did Cat have separate office space in Waukesha?"

"No. She worked at home. In fact, the office space there is quite cramped. Shabby, you know, particularly when compared with a business office. It's a converted warehouse. They sandblasted the exterior and put flowerboxes in the industrial-type windows, as if that would make a difference. They always said the home office was satisfactory, but I wish they'd move into something more, uh, something that looks better. We're representing God, you know."

"What was Cat's salary? Can ye tell me?"

"No. I don't know. I don't do well with figures. I never see the books, or help with them. I don't like computers. But then, Jules isn't much interested in Scripture, not nearly as much as he ought to be. We balance each other, you see. Different parts of the body serving separate functions. First Corinthians 12. Jules takes care of money matters."

"On the road?"

"All the time."

Tom frowned. "Meself understood that Persis hires an accounting firm."

"Jules goes over the books and things before the accountants get them."

"Be ye sure, lad?"

"Yes, I'm sure. He'll rag on me whenever I spend money, as if I could keep this branch of the ministry flowing without it."

Joe leaned forward and poked Turk. "Join me for some fun and games. Harley, I'd like a copy of that tape when he's through."

Turk stood up and stretched. "Where we going?"

"Bring in Jules and Persis Magen. They both know what's going on, and now we're gonna find out. Her prayers to fly to Riverside just got scotched for good."

TATTLETALES, TATTLETALES

For one reason or another, Joe found himself up around Flagstaff a couple times a year. There among the ponderosa pine he always marveled at how the heat beat down on you from above only. The green trees absorbed most of the lateral warmth and reflected only a little. Here in the desert around Phoenix, the heat came at you from everywhere—top, bottom and all sides at once, as the brilliant sun bounced off the ground and rocks and pavement and buildings.

Joe stood in the very middle of the oven of asphalt outside the motel. He was getting broiled on all sides, from the top of his head to the soles of his feet, and it wasn't yet eleven in the morning. Today was going to be a toaster.

Because of Jules' low opinion of blacks, Joe would let Turk do all the talking. He stood by Rocinante's front bumper as Turk knocked.

"Who is it?" Jules' muffled voice sounded sleepy.

"Ron Turcatto. Remember me? May we speak to you a minute?"

"You're one of those policemen." The voice sounded instantly more wakeful.

"Yeah, but I try not to dress like it."

"Not yet! I'm not ready yet!"

Turk muttered, "Forgot. He doesn't understand humor."

Joe stepped in against the wall beside the door.

The door opened, but Jules stayed inside the threshold. "What do you want?"

"We stopped to see Persis but she's not there and the room's locked. Any idea where she went? What her schedule is?"

"Ask the policemen watching her."

"They don't know. Apparently she slipped off somewhere."

"You said *we*. Who's with you?"

"Joe Rodriguez."

"Where's Tom? What do you really want? Why are there two of you, if you only want to talk to Persis?"

"Routine. We always come in matched sets." Turk glanced at Joe and cleared his throat. "Uh, Mr. Robinson, would you step out here, please, and come with us? We'd like to talk to . . ."

"I told you so! I knew you weren't here for her!"

A movement out in the parking lot caught Joe's eye. A woman, fiftyish and cheerfully chubby, was crossing between cars, and walking a dog. She paused by a camper, checked in both directions and stepped forward, the dog trotting at her side. It was a cute little mutt, a cocker spaniel the color they call apricot.

Joe heard the door whistle, swinging shut. Turk slammed into it *whack!* and it reversed directions. A blur whipped past Joe and shot out into the parking lot.

Wild-eyed, Jules grabbed the little lady with the dog and clutched her as a child would hide behind a blanket. He crooked his elbow around her neck.

"I'll break her back! I'll strangle her if you don't go away! Go find Persis. She's the one!"

The dog yapped and tugged at its leash.

Turk should be ten feet off to the side by now, moving out to divide Jules' attention between two diverging foci. Instead he just stood there like a lump. Joe appreciated all over again what a wonderful partner Tom Flaherty was.

Joe spread his hands wide. "What's the beef, Jules? Persis told me her staff was ready to help in any way possible, and that's you. We need your help. What's the problem?"

"Leave me alone. And tell that dog to go away." The lady's voice shook only a little. "Taffy. Sit."

The dog plopped to sitting, its silky bottom bobbing nervously on the asphalt. Joe caught the lady's eye and gave her the dog trainer's universal hand signal to lie down. It took her only a moment to gather her wits and courage. Suddenly she dropped like a sack of stones, melting out from under the crook of Jules' arm.

Even before she started to move, Joe was lunging forward. Jules hesitated, perplexed, and stared at the empty curve of his elbow. He turned and bolted but Joe was on him. Jules, the fop, was ridiculously easy to send sprawling.

"Bad choice, Jules." Joe planted his good foot on the man's neck.

"I didn't mean to do that."

"Of course."

"Let me up! The pavement is burning me!"

Joe kept him pinned down while Turk cuffed him. He stepped aside and Turk yanked the gawky young man to his feet. Jules had been right. His cheek sported a bright first-degree burn.

Joe watched them walk over to the cruiser. Then he spent an extra five minutes getting the lady's name and address and statement, praising her dog and her quick wit in equal proportions, and learning Taffy's ancestry, preferences and cute little mannerisms. It was time well spent. When they parted, the lady was beaming. Just wait until the girls hear about this!

Good. But one cheerful lady doesn't balance out a cruiser full of sullen cops and a suspect. Joe's headache was coming back.

Like planes stacked over Sky Harbor during rush hour, cops were hovering over the torture chamber. Tom had just finished an unusually long session with Henry Barbrie. Gabe Bisset from Vice was working a coke dealer in there now, and two robbery detectives were marking time, waiting for a chance at it.

Joe sat Jules down in the only room left, a dingy, barren cubicle with gray walls and a chipped wooden table. Across the hall in the lounge, he knew

Turk and the guys were turning on the TV monitor.

A surreptitious hand signal to Tom over by the pop machine was enough to agree with him on a "whoa partner" approach. Joe enjoyed this particular scam because it almost always worked. Besides, it was easy. He would be called upon to act increasingly cranky and hostile, and right now he felt very cranky and hostile, in no mood to be nice. Joe more or less pushed Jules into a chair and sat down opposite him.

Tom stepped into the room and closed the heavy door. He sipped at a can of black cherry soda.

Jules licked his lips, staring at the can. "Can I have one of those?"

Tom was saying, "Surely, lad" but Joe's voice overrode him. "Forget it."

Jules perched on the edge of his chair, grim and fidgety.

Joe sat back and glared at Jules. "I'm starting to get a little bored with you, boofhead. That business out in the parking lot was uncool. Everything you've been doing and saying is uncool. I don't like having to mess around with brainless clowns."

"I didn't mean to do that. I got scared. I didn't mean it."

"You don't think, either." Joe put an edge on his voice. "The last service on your car, they wrote the mileage on the door sticker. Lube and oil change, plugs and points. We did a little simple arithmetic on your present mileage and there's no way you drove that car to Riverside and back. So just where were you on the days you were supposed to be in California?"

"I did too go to Riverside. I set up all the arrangements there. That's my job. I do my job."

"Not in the company car you didn't."

"Don't yell at me like that. I'm not a common criminal. You treat me right or I don't cooperate, regardless of what Persis promised."

Joe pitched his voice a few decibels higher. "I'm sick of walking on eggs with you, pansy. You know things we want to know, and I'm done with trying to avoid ruffling your feathers while you sit there and spout racial slurs."

"Joe, lad, back off." Tom plunked into the chair at Joe's right and laid his arms across the table between them. He cooed, smooth as glass. "Now, Joe, I don't mind saying, meself is equally sick of constantly having to make apology for ye to the review board when they hear the complaints. Just calm yourself down, eh? Go slug the pop machine and have yourself a cola. Walk around the block or something. Calm yourself."

Joe half rose, nose to nose with the pallid Jules. "Calm down in a pig's eye! You know what this creep did a couple minutes ago? You sit in a nice cool building while I roll around on the hot asphalt correcting this boffo's mistakes. He's gonna cooperate now or I'll pull his scalp down over his belly button."

"But Joe, lad . . ."

"Stay outta my way. I'm gonna wring answers outta this dork."

"Aye, lad, aye! But after you've cooled off. Ye cannot be trusted when you're this upset, ye know that. Remember what happened last time?" Tom lifted

Joe by an elbow and gently shoved him toward the door. "Ten minutes. Give yourself ten minutes. There's a good lad. Just ten minutes." With a pat on the shoulder Tom sent Joe out into the hall. The door whispered closed.

Joe smiled. Love it! He walked the twenty paces down to the lounge and stepped inside. As one, four detectives and Gretchen all stood up and applauded.

Gretchen seized his hand and pumped it vigorously. "Oscar quality, start to finish. Who needs Robert Redford, with you around?"

Harley grinned. "Smooth, Don. You had me believing it."

"Yeah, but is it working?" Joe moved around to where he could see the TV monitor comfortably and leaned against the wall.

"Like a Japanese houseboy. Listen to 'im!" Harley pointed to the screen.

Joe knew the part of Tom's spiel he had just missed. Tom would already have apologized profusely. Then he would have warned Jules about the danger — the actual physical danger — of getting crosswise of this wild and volatile half-breed. Perhaps they could cover the delicate questions quickly, before Joe got back.

Jules was shaking a little. "He's smaller than I am. I'm not afraid of him."

Tom's voice shook a bit. Beautiful. "He's two inches shorter than I too, and I'm scared white. Ye cannot know what he's like when his bile's really up. A terror, he is, and worth avoiding at any cost."

Gretchen gazed at the monitor, rapt, and clutched Joe's arm. "Gloriosky, he's a charmer, Joe!

Talk the skin right off a sausage."

"About this mileage business," Tom was purring. "He's right, ye know. Ye could not've driven to Riverside and back. I know ye take your job seriously and I know ye do it right. So ye made all the arrangements by phone, aye? Or did ye fly?"

"I don't like to fly."

"Ah. By phone."

Jules nodded. "I was in Phoenix the whole time, at a different motel. Why should I waste time and money driving when I can confirm all the arrangements with a couple dollars worth of phone calls?"

"That's right, lad! Good stewardship."

Jules brightened instantly. "Yes! Precisely."

"And what were ye doing exactly during your spare time here in Phoenix?"

"Just hanging around the motel." Jules shrugged his puny shoulders. "Not this motel. Another one, on the north side of town. Then I moved down to this one after a couple days."

"Just hanging around."

"There weren't any good movies playing; I mean, like Disney or something. The old Disney movies, not that new stuff. So I watched TV and did a few things."

"What things?"

"Well, I went to the zoo a couple times. I like their tiger enclosure. It's impressive, like the tigers themselves. And the Indian Museum, but I didn't stay long there. I don't much like Indians. And there's a place called Rawhide north of town. But mostly I just hung around the room."

"Now this money problem between you and

Cat—the financial arrangement that Rodriguez was touching upon the other time. Do ye think ye can explain it to me quickly, before he gets back? Mayhap I can head him off."

The gangling accountant pressed his lips together. Tom made inconspicuous brow-mopping movements.

"That means Jules is sweating," Joe translated. "Sweat doesn't show up on the monitor; the camera can't pick it up."

Gretchen leaned against him. "You two have this down to a science. I'm impressed."

Tom scrunched himself down in his chair, making himself as distant and nonthreatening as possible.

Jules cleared his throat. "Cat was getting payments from Persis. I don't know why. Blackmail, obviously. I didn't see why they should be doing things like that and I get nothing. I'm a more diligent servant than Cat was. I don't get paid at all when we're in Waukesha, you know. So I asked for part. So Cat would give me a third of the payoff. I wanted half, but she threatened to get nasty, so I decided a third is good enough. But the payments got higher, so my part was more."

Tom nodded sympathetically. "And after all you've done for them too. So that figure we see in the books under the heading of Cat's office rent— that's the payment, aye? Cat took two-thirds of it and yourself one-third. Monthly?"

"Yes. Monthly."

"Is that the only entry that was falsified, do ye know? I mean to say, might Cat have been raking off from a couple different entries? Perhaps two or three?"

"I checked as much as I could, but I couldn't tell exactly,"

"What did Persis think about your desire to be included?"

"I don't think Cat mentioned it to her, and I didn't. I doubt she knew about the arrangement between Cat and me."

"Why do ye think Cat didn't blab? Weren't they close?"

"I threatened to reveal Cat's past to Persis if she caused trouble, you know?"

"Ah, yes, Cat's record. Don't ye think Persis already knew about it?"

"No. She always talks about Cat like she was some pure and holy nun. She wasn't. Oh my no."

"Aye. Thanks to your tipoff, we pieced together Cat's whole record. We certainly appreciate your help on that."

"You know, Marie has a spoiled past too. And a baby once. A bastard. But she wouldn't tell me much about it."

"We found all that stuff, aye."

"And Henry. He got arrested once. Probably more than once." Jules leaned forward, tete-a-tete. "Henry's a pickpocket, did you know that? A good one. Oh, he won't admit it, of course, but he is. I know. Just like I know about Cat and Marie."

"Ye don't say. But Cat seems the worst of the pack, aye?"

"Mm hmm."

"Ever use Cat's typewriter? I understand she got

fair upset if someone used it. Silly, that. It's an old clunker."

"No. I don't type much."

"Mm." Tom shifted. "Meself has so much trouble typing, when the reports pile up I try to date a stenographer. Not at all?"

"I took typing in school, but I don't like it. Most accounting is on computer now, as you know, but I do books the right way. By hand. Then you know what you have and some machine doesn't just swallow up all your figures. If one of those virus things strikes their computer, they'll be on their knees thanking me. Or a power failure or something."

Harry Wallace came sauntering in and parked close beside Joe. Joe felt like a slice of bologna between slices of Wiemer and Wallace. He crowded Gretchen aside to give Harry room.

Gretchen murmured, "Gate crasher."

Joe glanced at Harry. "So what'd you find in Jules' room?"

Harry shrugged. "Nothing much. He planning to get married?"

"Hasn't mentioned any lucky girls. Why?"

"Bride books. Must have thirty or forty bride magazines in a stack. Latest is three months old. And a Monkey Ward catalog."

"Current?"

"Winter. Almost current."

Joe watched Jules digressing on Marie's past. He didn't know as much about it as Joe and Tom did. "Any favorite parts? Harry?"

"In the catalogue? Yeah. Ladies' lingerie. That section's frazzled."

"Porn?"

"Nope. Nothing, not even soft stuff." Harry's voice trailed away, his attention wrapped up in the monitor. "Gonna hold him?"

"Don't know yet."

"His place seems clean. Didn't find a 6 by 9 linen tablet, either, or anything like you were mentioning. Nothing outta character for him."

"Probably let him go, then. Give him a scare first."

On the TV screen Tom was scratching his right sideburn.

"That's my cue to go back. See you around." Joe lurched erect and walked down to the cubicle. He arranged his face and went in. For the next few minutes he would fuss and fume as Tom cooed and purred, assuring him all the bases had been covered. Jules would fill in a few more details, none significant.

Joe realized they had to spend some time to wind down the act, complete the performance. But he was anxious to get on to the next step, the next person, the key to this puzzle—Persis Magen.

Persis Speaks

Joe knocked at Persis' motel door. Tom paced back and forth on the walkway behind him. Joe was hungry enough to eat cactus and he knew Tom had less tolerance for late lunches than he. Chen had said she was back. They would scoop her up, haul her down . . .

"Just a moment." Persis sounded bright and cheerful as ever. The door swung open. She was brushing her hair, the long gray mane clasped in one hand and her hairbrush in the other.

A slight, brief shadow flickered across her face and she returned to her mien of good cheer. "Why, good afternoon, gentlemen! Have you had lunch?"

"Not yet." Tom perched by Joe's shoulder, smiling. Joe would not have said that. They were going to pick up fast food and take it and Persis to a cubicle—a dreary one.

"Please, may I treat you? I was just going to lunch myself. Come in. I'll only be a moment." She wheeled and disappeared off into the bathroom. Her voice continued, a few decibels louder. "I was supposed to attend a luncheon with a ladies' group this afternoon and begged off. I have reached my saturation point for socializing with strangers." She reappeared, her hair in a neat, loose bun. "Somewhere nice and quiet and unbusy."

The plan, Joe reminded himself, was to cart this lady downtown for interrogation.

Tom's voice flowed like liquid silver. What was he up to? "Mrs. Magen, milady, we know just the place. Restful and quiet and splendid food."

Joe poked him. "Not that Basque place again."

"Ah, my, no, Jose. Thai House. That is, Mrs. Magen, if ye fancy Oriental food."

"My favorite."

Tom piloted her out the door toward Rocinante. "There be two of 'em; the one on the west side makes ye feel like you're in the middle of a high school band. But the other makes a quiet meadow seem like Camelback and Seventh."

"The other one *is* at Camelback and Seventh." Joe slid into the driver's seat.

"Eh, ye see? It works." Tom ushered Persis gallantly into the passenger side.

Once there, Joe saw anew the dark underbelly of celebrity status. People stopped to stare at Persis Magen as she climbed out of the car at Thai House. They whispered to each other. A couple started to approach and Joe scowled them into turning aside. Imagine being under scrutiny like this every time you stepped out in public. No thanks.

Tom did pick his restaurants well. Thai House was sparsely populated this noon, quiet and dark. They chose a little round table in a secluded nook. Tom made certain he sat directly across from Persis. Joe felt the distinct impression of being dead weight, simply along for the ride and the food. Very well. This was Tom's forte. Let him do his thing.

Persis and Tom discussed the abortion issue clear through the appetizer. When was Tom going to get to the pertinent stuff? Joe began to feel impatient.

Finally. "Mrs. Magen, we've some unsettling questions—nagging problems if ye will. Now I'm sorry to mix business with the pure pleasure of this delightful time, but we've many loose ends to wrap up and precious little time for the wrapping."

"I hope you're not apologizing for doing your job."

"No, but I apologize for the rotten timing. Rotten but necessary."

"I flit in and out so much it's hard to catch me. Your timing is excellent."

"Then shall we start at the very beginning? The second night of your meetings and afterward . . ."

"When someone tried to shoot Marie?"

"The very time. Where were ye those four hours, exactly?"

"Exactly?" She smiled. "Lost."

"Lost."

"I walk a lot. You see, I suffer from arthritis. An osteoarthritis, specifically. When it starts kicking up, I find that walking helps. That's why I sometimes pace back and forth on the dais, like a lion in the zoo. Hip discomfort. Also, walking helps me think. That night I took what was meant to be simply a short, private little walk. I ended up on curving residential streets with more cul-de-sacs per square yard than I've ever seen. Since the stars were too obliterated to navigate by and I didn't know the streets, I was nearly four hours getting back."

"Why?" Joe asked. "Why go to such lengths to dump a man whose job is to protect you?"

"Some people can't stand to be alone. Most don't care. But I find it intolerable to be with others constantly. For reasons of finance we usually pair up in lodging, driving, etc. I need aloneness. Not one man tagging along as company. Alone. And at Valley that afternoon, I was not trying to give you the slip. A woman asked my advice and prayer support regarding an unsaved relative and I took her aside. I often do that."

"I'll take that at face value, for the moment. But you gave Harry the slip like a practiced professional."

"I am a practiced professional, Mr. Rodriguez."

So she was back to the formal term of address, the honorific. Not all the good cheer in her voice had erased her distrust. She continued. "I got my training in Africa and my internship in Vietnam."

"Specify, if ye would." Frequently Tom feigned interest to bring a subject along. Joe could tell by his tone of voice that this interest was genuine.

"My husband was a missionary to Zaire—the Congo back then—right after our marriage. We were accused of espionage and declared enemies by the provisional government in our district. We instantly became very good at staying underground. We remained in that district finishing the work Sam had started—sneaking around, hiding, meeting clandestinely with the believers. The village magistrate thought we had fled seven months before we actually left."

"Your husband's work exactly?"

"Establishing an indigenous church, a testimony to Christ among the Africans themselves. His work was fruitful. I still receive mail from the assembly in Nkunga. Healthy and strong."

"And what was your own part in his work? Secretarial? Garbage collection? The real power behind the throne?"

Persis chuckled. "Medical to an extent. I have a practical nursing diploma. Mostly record-keeping and secretarial. Some counseling."

"You're trained in all that?"

"High school business—typing, but I'm not good at it, Gregg Simplified pothooks, basic accounting. I ignored all that precious training and kept the books my way. Actually, I found the business training of real use in college."

"Doctorate in psychology, aye. Quite a lot of college, with a nursing diploma to boot."

"I obtained the doctorate after we returned from Africa."

"And ye write out your sermons longhand."

"By preference. I can think better; I write much faster than I can type; and I can write around corners, in margins and down the sides. You can't do that on a typewriter."

"And it's quieter. Don't forget the incessant

pickety-pick. How about one of those dandy little portable computers? Laptops? Word processors?"

"I realize this is the computer age, but I refuse to enter it. My staff and organization use computers, of course."

"Ye mentioned practical experience in Vietnam."

"I went over with a medical advisory group during the war and remained behind after the pullout. We were involved with an orphanage outside Hue. There was this charming little fellow—a double agent, no doubt—who forged me a phony passport and visa for a modest sum. I speak French well enough that they never caught on I was American."

Tom's eyebrows popped up. "An exciting life! Why be ye not doing that sort of thing yet?"

She shrugged. "The Cong needed the particular acre the orphanage was on and evicted us. We dispersed the children as best we could and hauled ourselves out of there. I have a saturation point for socializing; I also have a saturation point for derring-do."

"In other words, you've had enough of thrills."

"The fastest things in Waukesha are the little numbers spinning on the gas pump, and I love it. Must be getting old."

Joe interrupted. "Are you still in contact with many Vietnamese in this country?"

"A few. None associated with the orphanage."

Joe pondered a moment. "How about Larry Jennings? In contact with him?"

"Glory Desert Assembly? Not directly. Reverend Blanchard—you met him at Valley that day—the gray moustache—knows him. I believe he supplied some personnel, counselors. But no. I haven't worked with him directly."

"Does he have any Southeast Asians in his organization?"

"Not that I know of, but I wouldn't know."

"And you wouldn't have put a bug in his ear about launching a telephone campaign on your behalf."

"A what? No. We don't do telemarketing, either."

The waiter brought the main course in half a dozen delicate dishes. Tom waited until he left.

"Ye be a quick and clever lady, able to live by your wits. Ye could be lying through your teeth this very moment and making it sound ex cathedra. How do I know you're telling the truth, now or any other time?"

"Very perceptive of you, Mr. Flaherty. You're right. I'm extremely good at passing falsehood off as, excuse the phrase, gospel truth. Excuse another phrase, you have to take my word on faith—I do assure you I'm giving you honest, truthful answers."

"Taking someone's word for anything is not the policeman's way, Mrs. Magen." Joe held her eye. "Would you object to a polygraph treatment of certain key questions?"

"They say a polygraph can't be beaten—at least they try to convince you thus. I can beat it, Mr. Rodriguez. It's a matter of record. They put me through the wringer when I returned from Nam, and I successfully fouled up their polygraph. Contradictory responses on identical questions. I was feeling playful at the time, and fed up with the overly self-important investigators. Which, I hasten to add, you two are not."

"You didn't answer my question."

"I would not object, despite the fact your results would be inconclusive."

How could such a warm and witty lady be so cold and calculating? Was it her manner, her choice of words or what? Joe picked at his lunch until he tasted the dish with the yellow chilies. He dug right in.

Tom broke the silence. "The newest wing at Sky Harbor—the terminal annex with the red carpeting—how do ye like it?"

"It sounds very pretty, but I'm not into touring airports."

"You're saying you've never been there?"

"That's right."

"Mrs. Magen, we've proof ye were." Tom should be asking Persis about *her* ability to lie convincingly? His tone of voice had Joe believing that one for a moment.

She smiled. "Your source is spurious, Mr. Flaherty. I've not been there."

"Perhaps only in the parking garage."

She looked at him strangely and let it pass. "I don't tour parking lots, either."

Joe watched for some sign, any little hint, that the question bothered her or put her on her guard. Nothing. "The day after the bombings you asked Marie to return to Waukesha. Why?"

"Her nerves were frazzled."

"You thought she might be the target?"

"Possibly."

"You thought she might be the bomber?"

"Impossible."

"You are the bomber and you hoped that if she fled to Waukesha, she would look so suspicious as to draw attention away from you."

She stayed cool as Nome on a winter day. "Interesting thesis. I'm constantly impressed by your professionalism, both of you. It's your job to explore all the probabilities, I realize. But you come up with such intriguing twists. I never would have thought of that."

Joe smiled. "There are other suppositions. For example, Cat threatens blackmail of some sort. You must silence her before she causes you embarrassment or becomes an onerous financial burden. The payments are escalating, getting steeper. You yourself prepare threatening notes to use as a smoke screen, typing four or more of them on Cat's own machine. You send them to yourself, spacing them at logical intervals. How expedient that one of them just happens to be waiting for us in your wastebasket the day she dies. You send the fourth note after her death—the one that shows that Cat was not the intended victim at all, and diverts us from seeking a motive for her murder. We concentrate, erroneously, on finding the one who would harm Persis Magen."

Persis studied his face a long time. "And you mentioned blackmail as a motive?"

"The money dispensed under the heading of Cat's office space. I'd appreciate your side of the story on that."

She mulled her answer awhile. "When a believer

makes a financial gift to the organization, he assumes the money will be used exclusively for God's work and that it will not be wasted. We are stewards of that gift and are called to be true to the giver's purpose."

"In other words, no company funds for private use."

"Precisely. Private inurement."

"That was what did the Bakkers in, right?"

"Yes. And, of course, we operate under the unsleeping eye of the Internal Revenue Service, so we take extra pains to keep an honest accounting.

"I don't know how deeply you investigated Cat's past; thoroughly, I presume, since you also delved into Marie's. When Cat converted close to four years ago, she came under heavy satanic attack. Her most recent husband was in the process of divorcing her. Her baby was handicapped. Spina bifida. She couldn't be the full-time mother the child needed and support herself also. She appealed to me for help. She didn't expect financial aid, of course, but she sought counsel and perhaps suggestions as to where she might turn, what avenues I could see open to her.

"By God's providence my secretary had just retired. Cat had no experience along that line, but she possessed a remarkably well-organized mind. You could see it immediately as you talked to her. And she was splendidly poised. Articulate. I hired her as my personal secretary. She operated partly out of my office and mostly out of her home."

"Where and what was her home?"

"A modest apartment within walking distance of

the office. She paid her rent out of her salary. She also paid part of her son's medical expenses. Certain national funds helped defray some of those costs. And what medical costs were not picked up otherwise were paid for under the heading 'Cat's office.' "

Joe glanced at Tom.

The Irishman sat gaping, enthralled. "Surely that be blatant misuse of money earmarked for the work of God, Mrs. Magen."

"Not in the least. We are guilty of absolutely no wrongdoing, either legally or ethically. Her child belongs to God, as does she. Both are part of the organization. Incidentally, Eric—that's his name—will still be cared for by the organization. The child has a need we can meet, a need that can be met from no other source."

"Aye." Tom nodded. "But your books—your records are a lie. Did ye not say yourself, 'Satan is the father of lies'? You're perpetrating falsehood by crediting that money to a fictitious expenditure. Ye see me meaning?"

"I didn't originate 'father of lies.' Jesus did. We talked about that very point a long time. If it's Eric's medical costs, why not say so? But my advisers believed that such an entry would invite criticism where none is justified, so I went along with them. However, now that Cat's dead, we'll label it as it ought to be labeled."

Tom nodded. "I see. Your advisers took the position that the wise man does not tie his shoes in his neighbor's melon patch."

Joe had to think about that one a moment.

Persis didn't. "Exactly. I reiterate that the entry is totally ethical. Cat converted over half of her apartment into office space, so that she might work at home. She did not take that space off her income tax. So you see, the organization received the space it was paying for."

"A separate office."

"Yes."

"How was the money paid?" Joe forgot about the chilies.

"A check made out to Cat from the organization account."

"The amount increased."

"Eric needed a different and somewhat more expensive mode of treatment. Kidney problems."

Joe leaned back. He wasn't sure where to go next.

Tom picked up the ball. "Jules arranges your accounts before your accounting firm gets them, as I understand it. Was he responsible for juggling the books about?"

Persis smiled and polished off the last of her plateful. "Dear Jules. He's certain our finances will get all messed up without him. He drifts in and out of the Waukesha office and, as you say, arranges the accounts—he thinks. He refuses to work at a terminal. Pencils in things on hard copies. It's not a significant contribution. And no, he didn't juggle anything."

"But he questioned the entry about office rent."

"Yes. We explained it to him and he said no more about it."

"Oh? And you're telling us no part of the payment went to him?"

The lady never blinked. "None that I know of. You mean hush money?"

"The term's been bandied about quite a bit lately."

"There's nothing to hush up."

Tom hadn't touched his food in five minutes. When he forgot to eat he was rapt indeed. "Jules changed his name when he reached majority. Do ye know what his name was previously?"

"He's always been Jules Robinson to us."

"Mrs. Magen," asked Joe, "you visited Marie as soon as we arrested her. Did she know about his payment business before then?"

"She was neither interested in the books nor privy to them. Apparently she heard a whiff of something about it. She had no details. I doubt Cat mentioned it to her. Jules might have."

"And ye both used the device of her confession," said Tom, "the end being that ye get to Riverside on time."

"Sounds heartless to you, no doubt. Marie's willing to make the sacrifice. She's no stranger to jails, you know. And I'll be back as soon as I can, to see to her needs and comfort. We're both certain you have nothing solid to make it stick. It's a temporary artifice, as you say, to get me on the road again."

"*Heartless* is an understatement." Joe knew what happens to a woman booked on a serious charge. She is stripped, searched, sent through the showers, sprayed with louse killer and searched in her private parts. It had never mattered too much before. You arrest a hooker here, a shoplifter there, an occasional hysterical woman who just blasted her lover. But Marie . . .

Tom and Persis drifted into a discussion of the newspaper and TV play this case was getting, with its impact on attendance at her meetings. Joe sifted other prospects. Little details nagged at him, insisting in his ear that they were not so small. But which signified heavily? He was uncertain. He waited for a break in the dialogue. Finally Tom shut up long enough to finish his lunch.

Joe dived into the breach of silence. "Mrs. Magen, I understand that at one time Jules was enamored with Cat, at least to an extent. Is that true?"

"Probably, Mr. Rodriguez. She was strikingly attractive and not just physically. The purity of her Christian walk too. But then, he became enamored, as you put it, of most girls sooner or later. He was equally attracted to Marie for a time. And to a little blond stenographer who worked in a law office across the hall from us. We referred to that one as his water cooler romance."

"Not to his face."

"Of course not. He would have taken it wrongly. His sense of humor is not well developed."

Joe could drink to that. His questions had not achieved a thing. Instead of solving all those raucous, clamoring details, he had simply added more to the pile. And the more he tried to sort this wayward melange of detail, the more he thought about Marie.

GLORY!

J oe deeply distrusted security systems, and yet in a sense he was one. Along with electrified fences, Doberman pinschers, and burglar alarms, policemen are security, protecting property and people from each other. That made him part of the scene here. Doberman pinschers, however, do not solve mysterious and complex crimes, and that's where all the fun lies.

He pulled up at the security gate identified only by its street number, 32554. A buffer zone of fifteen-foot oleanders, made dense by constant shearing, protected the lot from traffic noise and artfully hid a cyclone fence topped with razor wire. It also kept the two dogs from roaming, no doubt. They paced back and forth on the other side, barking. From the outside looking in, this Brother Larry Jennings appeared as paranoid as a drug dealer.

From beyond the oleanders Joe heard an approaching motor. Its engine quit. A burly gentleman in a dark suit and ponytail stepped out from behind the guard kiosk just inside the gate. Joe distrusted men in ponytails too.

In fact, he didn't trust Dobermans worth diddly either, especially if he was in his Midget. A good-sized Doberman has to look down to see you in an open Midget, its muzzle right in your face. Today he was driving Rocinante, fortunately, and Rocinante could choke the dogs to death on exhaust fumes. Wordlessly he displayed his badge at his open window.

Wordlessly the pony stepped into the kiosk. The gate swung open silently. The dogs romped all around Rocinante, barking and feinting at Joe's window as he drove in. The pony called them away and Joe continued around the curved cement drive to Brother Larry's house.

The devil twinkling in his eye, Tommy had begged off this meeting; had other investigative work of a pressing nature, he claimed apologetically. Joe understood. He might feel a little uncomfortable around these hypocrites, but Tommy had every right to feel a whole lot worse. Tommy's trophy case held everything from a Miss Arizona to a former dean of women at a small local college.

Brother Larry's home sprawled across a couple acres of carefully tended "natural" desert. A beautiful Santa Fe style hacienda with stucco arches and red tiled roof announced that the income of its owner extended to the high end of six figures.

In his mind, Joe imagined Brother Larry as a big,

oily southern guy in a leisure suit. He pictured a sanctimonious manner based on the radio voice he and Tommy had listened to this morning on Hour of Glory. He would not have guessed the stringent security measures out at the gate or here at the front door. The windows were barred and the door armed with locks, a speaker box, and peepholes on two levels.

He got out of Rocinante with no little trepidation. How obedient were those Dobermans, exactly?

A quiet and composed Southeast Asian woman answered his knock and ushered him inside. Her soft, unaccented voice seemed to smile. "Brother Larry is expecting you, officer."

Joe thanked her and followed her through the open, airy living room to offices in the back. The upholstered furnishings were all done in light southwestern colors. He looked for black Doberman hairs or smudges on the corners of the chairs and sofas. Apparently the dogs didn't come in here. The place didn't smell like dogs, either. And Brother Larry's air-conditioning bill had to be a couple hundred a month.

Behind a desk the size of a soccer field, Brother Larry Jennings rose to meet Joe and extended a hand. The good preacher stood five-feet seven at most, skinny and jug-eared like Ross Perot, and he wore blue jeans and a T-shirt. The T-shirt didn't even have any cute motto printed on it. Whatever Joe expected, this sure wasn't it. He shook two-handed.

Brother Larry waved toward the overstuffed chair beside his desk. "Be seated, officer. My secretary tells me you have a few questions taking half an hour or so." His sonorous voice was much stronger than the slight, pipsqueak body would indicate.

"Probably not that long." Joe sat. Marvelously soft chair. "You are aware that I'm working on the Magen case."

"Yes, I recognized your name. Did you happen to listen to the program this morning?"

Joe nodded.

Brother Larry sat back in his own oversized naugahyde chair. "I'll be very bold and ask what you thought of it."

"The music was wonderful. I've always really liked the old-time gospel songs."

The tiny eyes between those huge ears pierced right through Joe. The man's face relaxed a bit, and he smiled. It was an "aha" sort of look, and Joe wondered what revelation the fellow had just received, what trumpet call from on high.

Joe had in mind several questions he planned to open with. He scrubbed them and started off on an entirely different track. "Permit me to be very bold as well. You've just reached some sort of decision. I'm curious what it is."

The eyebrows raised slightly. The face relaxed again. "Astute. I've come to a couple of decisions, since we're both speaking boldly. I am interviewed by all manner of people—writers and reporters, mostly. Never a policeman before. Some are very good and most are very bad. I can give them any line I want and they buy it. My decision just now is that I'm not going to be able to buffalo you. Probably not even be evasive. I asked a leading question and you answered forthrightly, with no hesitation. My analysis at the end of the newscast today was fairly uncomplimentary toward your police department, so you were very diplomatic in the bargain; you avoided reference to that and instead commented on a positive element. That tells me something, you see; so does the fact that you seem to be able to read my face well."

"Yours is an expressive face."

"Yours is not."

Joe propped his elbows on the chair arms and made an A out of his fingertips. Was the jockeying and circling done now? He hoped so. "I'm not here to talk about your commentaries. I appreciate that they're your personal opinion, to which you are welcome. But I am interested in data. In assembling your newscast, you are obviously privy to more than just the department news releases. You have sources, in other words."

"You're not expecting me to divulge them, I hope."

"No, but I do need leads to pursue, avenues to investigate. I am hoping that with your news-gathering—your ear to the ground, as it were—you might be able to help me."

"Are you asking this of other newsgathering sources also? The newspapers, for instance?"

"No. You obviously have access to Persis Magen's inner sanctum and they do not. Also, they don't understand Persis' mind-set, the way she thinks, and I suspect you do."

"I don't think I can help you."

Joe let that ride a moment, let the silence move in. Silence usually tends to make most interviewees antsy. It didn't seem to bother Brother Larry. Joe continued, "Your analysis this morning suggested you believe that police are engaged in a pogrom against the forces for good. An epic battle of good versus evil. I understand you've said that more than once in the last few days. Several of your own followers have informed me that if I'm not on the side of good, I am abetting evil. The same is true of you. If you can aid the forces for righteousness, Mr. Jennings, now is the time to do it."

"I don't believe you are righteous. I believe you are using this case in an attempt to bring glory to a police department that needs all the good PR it can get. Heaven knows, your reputation has been somewhat tarnished lately. I don't mean your reputation personally, of course. The department's."

"And if you're wrong? If we really are trying to find the truth and see justice served?"

"I don't think I'm wrong."

"Men of firm opinions never do. I repeat, what if?"

"Then I am opposing truth." Brother Larry wagged his head. "I'm sorry. I still don't think I can help you." He started to rise.

Joe remained seated, kept himself relaxed. "You claimed I am about to arrest Persis Magen. What is the basis for that claim?"

"Privileged sources." He sat down again, but he had lost his casual air.

"Not the sources. The facts."

"Nothing you could construe as a lead to follow."

Joe wished Tommy were here. Tom could say downright irritating things and have the listener smiling as he said them. Joe tended to merely irritate. "May I suggest that you had no basis for the claim, but it sounded better than the truth—that the police were simply investigating. If we're doing nothing more than working on the case, the battle of good versus evil appears to be on a back burner, if on the stove at all, and your thesis loses credence."

The radio-trained voice rose a few decibels. "I do not manufacture the news, officer."

"In your commentary this morning, you claim Marie Kabrhan is innocent but the cops have to arrest somebody in order to look good, so a minion of Persis Magen is 'it.' Why are you convinced of her innocence?"

"I spoke with her personally. I said on the air that I did. If you were listening you'd know that."

"I heard you. But according to personnel at the jail, Marie received no visitors."

"You're on a first-name basis with her."

The change of direction very nearly unhorsed him. Joe ignored the comment and stuck to his point. "Nor did she receive lengthy phone calls. I'm not impugning your honesty. I'm trying to learn the basis of your assumptions."

"It certainly sounds like you're impugning my honesty. I told you, I'm not going to divulge any sources, or even the information they provide. I can't help you."

"I understand that Glory Desert Assembly is not among the many churches taking part in Persis Magen's meetings. I would assume this is because of doctrinal differences. Do you know personally, or do you know about, any of her staff?"

The brother was obviously going to cut that one short too, but he remembered in time that this was an official police inquiry and not some news reporter out fishing. "I know Henry Barbrie personally. And no, he is not one of my sources. I haven't had contact with him in recent years."

"When and where did you meet him?"

"My ministry led to his conversion. I was in the Bay area up until two years ago."

"California."

The brother nodded. "San Jose. He worked for me for about six months. Interesting young man. Very much filled with the Holy Spirit."

"In what capacity did you employ him?"

"Security."

"He's half the size of your gentleman in the ponytail out there."

"He knows security procedures and weaponry. He did that kind of work before I hired him, and he served just fine. Then one day he turned in his resignation and moved home. I forget now which state. He's not a native Californian."

"Weaponry. Munitions? Explosives?"

"That kind of thing, yes."

"He's in town here and you say you've had no contact with him? Not even a 'hello' phone call?"

"You're impugning my honesty again."

"Just double-checking, making sure I understand."

"Of course. Now, is that all?"

Joe sighed audibly, a calculated move. "One other thing. You realize, Brother Larry, that the department's switchboard operators have replaced the picture of Saddam on their dartboard with a snapshot of me. And the homicide receptionist is ready to abandon her voodoo doll and stick her pins directly into me.

"Your listeners are doing as you requested, calling in by the hundreds, but it's getting you nowhere. It's only blocking the phone lines so that legitimate calls for aid and assistance are delayed. Your protest campaign is going to cause an innocent party's injury or death when the cops can't be reached in time."

"Your appeal tells me the call-in campaign is doing its job—letting you people know that we won't sit back while liberal atheists try to railroad a fellow believer."

"Too bad." Joe stood up. "What it's supposed to tell you is that you'll be facing a court injunction to clear our phone lines if the problem doesn't resolve itself immediately." He turned away, paused, and turned back to Brother Larry. "One other question. Why the tight security?"

"There was a day when religious leaders didn't have to worry about screwballs or homicidal maniacs. Those days are no more."

Joe studied the Navajo carpet a moment. "Couldn't agree with you more." He nodded to the man. "Good day, Mr. Jennings."

He left by the route he had come in, out through that cavernous living room, threading between sumptuous furnishings. He felt frustrated and angry and just plain ugly. The maid who had escorted him appeared out of nowhere to escort him out. He

gave her a smile and spoke a few civilized words—
it wasn't her fault her boss was a pompous little
donkey—and so did she. He stepped from air-conditioned cool into natural heat.

The solid oak door closed behind him. And a Doberman muzzle opened directly in front of him. The
dog snarled and threatened, his backup right beside
him and looking for a way to get around behind
Joe. They'd obviously been waiting there for him.

Joe stayed in the portal and yelled, "Hey, ponytail! Come get your dogs or I shoot them!"

No response. Rocinante sat thirty feet away.
Could Joe make a run for the car and get there in
one piece? For that matter, did he have to? He
knew enough to avoid looking either one of them in
the eye, but he didn't remember much else about
handling obstreperous guard dogs. The kids had
been badgering him for years to get a dog. He rather regretted resisting their pleas. At least he'd know
a little about how dogs think.

Acting like he belonged here, he stepped forward,
exuding a confidence he did not feel. He got maybe
ten feet before the snarling dog decided to lunge.
Joe lashed out with his good leg, the one he could
control better, and caught the mutt in the chops.
Already the dog's buddy had made a pass at Joe's
bad leg. The dog almost yanked his foot out from
under him, but he came away mostly with a mouth
full of pants leg.

Joe made a wild dive for Rocinante. He didn't
bother with a door; he belly flopped onto the hood
and hauled his legs up. The metal burned hot
against his skin. He kept right on scrambling until

he sat on the roof, his fanny pressed against the
light bar. He felt about as dignified as a two-year-
old in a sandbox.

His anger was building, burning, and nothing he
could tell himself would bank the fire. Livid beyond
reason, he pulled his gun and fired one at God. His
gunshot excited the dogs to a wild and furious spate
of barking.

The big oaken front door swung back and here
came the maid. She gaped wide-eyed for a moment.
"Major! Jupiter!"

Major and Jupiter paid no attention. She disappeared back inside, leaving the door hanging
open—a definite breach of security. Moments later
she came running back out, carrying two aluminum dog dishes.

"Major! Jupiter! Dindin!" She banged the dishes
together. The barking ceased. "Come in, right now.
Come!" She backed in the door. "Dindin."

With a few parting barks, the Dobies jogged in
the door, following their dishes. She stepped out
into the portal, tossed the dishes inside, and
slammed the door quickly.

She ran to Rocinante, her face tight with worry.
"I'm so sorry! I didn't know they were out here.
They stay down at the kiosk with Mark."

The motor scooter came roaring up. Ponytail
stared at Joe a moment and smirked. "Don't you
look glorious!"

Joe eased himself off the car roof and addressed
the maid. "Thanks for your service. I appreciate it."
He crossed to the motor scooter and let the anger
tighten his voice all it wanted to. "Why did Henry

Barbrie quit?"

"What...?"

"You heard me. You replaced him. Why did he quit?"

"Uh..." The ponytail looked confused. "He got into some kind of trouble and Mr. Jennings canned him. I dunno."

Joe watched his face a moment and couldn't see anything other than the sudden confusion. He grimaced. "I'll send a bill for the new slacks. Go open the gate for me." He slid into Rocinante's seat.

Ponytail swung aboard his scooter and wheeled it around down the drive.

Joe drove out behind him. Good glory, how he hated religion!

To Sleep ... Perchance to Dream

Joe? See you a minute?" Jerry Hocks stood by his office door. He was getting some salt in his pepper sideburns, and his face had a few lines now, but basically, the lieutenant looked as trim and young as when Joe entered the department nine years ago.

Joe detoured and stepped inside. Jerry closed the door. So this was going to be a personal discussion, and therefore probably not related to any of the cases in Joe's hopper. Jerry flopped into his chair and waved at the upholstered chair off the end of his desk.

Joe sat. He didn't want to sit around talking. He wanted to get on with his idea. He'd already called Harvey Spruce. It was all set up.

"How's it going?" Jerry watched him like a cat watches a mouse hole.

"Fine."

"The rangemaster says you qualified with either hand."

"That wasn't my idea. He asked me to."

"Because I requested it. And I bet you could take this conversation from here and run with it without my help."

Joe nodded. "The department's legal types are getting antsy again."

Jerry grimaced and bobbed his head. "You still don't have full strength back in either your arm or your leg. You're not up to snuff, Joe. You're not fit to be out on the street. They're afraid of the accident that's going to happen because of it, either to you or to someone else. Maybe a civilian with a good attorney."

"I've passed every test you stuck in front of me so far. I'm as fit as anyone else."

"On paper. But out on the street . . ."

"Jerry . . ." Joe stopped. They'd been through this a hundred times. So he'd take a new tack for once. "When I hired on they were in the middle of a 'we need more minority officers' craze."

"Right." Jerry paused. "We didn't have Englishmen on the force at all, and you're half English."

Joe snickered. "Correct. What everyone failed to notice is that I was as qualified then as any white, with enough college, enough part-time experience, and high enough scores across the board. I was still the minority hire, the guy who got ushered in because of my name."

"You're overstating it."

"I'm understating it. Then they suddenly discovered they didn't have enough minorities in the upper ranks. Bingo. Suddenly I'm a sergeant. It doesn't matter that I had as many years' experience as any white in the division when they tagged me for the promotion, and that I was among the best qualified. I was the minority promotion, the guy who got there in order to fill a quota."

"Come on, Joe, get off this 'poor me' racial stuff. You're the most racially neutral guy I know."

"I'm not poor-meing. I'm explaining some facts for you. Now there's another push on to shove some minorities upstairs. That's why Washington and Hanhouse are lieutenants, when they have half the experience you did when you moved up."

"Okay, I'll admit that much is right."

"And if I make lieutenant, I'll be pretty much off the street. That will ease the legal department's fears. And another minority makes good, satisfying the unspoken quota. Two birds with one stone."

"You forget the best part. Raise in pay."

"You forget the worst part, Jerry. I hate paperwork. It's the only thing you grouse about on my annual evaluation; I don't get the paperwork done. I like the job I have now. I enjoy matching wits with people who think they can play God and get away with it. I enjoy unraveling puzzles. I enjoy snooping around, digging up the facts. It's where the action is. It's what makes the job worth the danger and frustration. I'm not going to let myself get kicked upstairs to sit at a desk shuffling paper, and lose all that."

"They may kick you upstairs anyway, the noises the legal department's making."

"Then they have a personnel action on their

hands. I refuse to go."

An expletive burst out of Jerry and he almost never used them. "Why are you making this so hard?"

"I want to do what I want to do, and I don't want to do what I don't want to do. I wouldn't be any good at all as a lieutenant. I'm so lousy at being a sergeant I've asked everyone in the division to overlook my rank. I'm very good at investigation." He spread his hands. "Period."

"They're talking about shoving you out the door on a disability, Joe. And don't tell me they can't do it. They can. Then you'll be stuck with retirement pay based on what you're making now. You can't raise your kids on that. Get a couple years in as lieutenant and you can jack your retirement enough to put your kids through school."

Joe felt the frustration building again. *You act like you're looking out for my best interests, Jerry, and what you're really doing is pitching the department's party line. But I can't say that out loud.* Instead, he said, "Tommy and I make your division look good, Jerry. We consistently nail the perps and avoid embarrassing you or the force. You need all of that kind of people you can get. Don't mess yourself up."

Jerry grunted. "And that's the only reason you haven't been canned already. This is your last word?"

"Until you bring the subject up again and I have to repeat it."

Jerry stood up suddenly. "You have our tails covered adequately for this afternoon?"

"Harvey Spruce." Joe stood up and hang if his

right leg didn't almost buckle. Timing is everything. "Look on the bright side, Jerry. It's another minority."

Jerry sighed as he walked over and opened the door. "I don't want to hear the word again, understand? Don't rub it in my face."

Joe smiled. "I forget everything I just said. I'll let you know how this afternoon comes out."

Jerry nodded and turned away.

He didn't look at all pleased.

Gretchen Wiemer leaned against the water cooler in Tom Flaherty's squad room and watched the Irishman pace back and forth.

"Uncanny, Gretch. Nothing short of uncanny. We went out specifically to bring the lady in. Twenty minutes later we're sitting in Thai House like proper white folks, eating the special of the day. She's a charmer, she is. A charmer."

Speak for yourself, John. Gretchen smiled. Tom looked cuter than ever when he was perplexed. Part of his appeal was his reputation as a gallant and enthusiastic ladykiller. On the other hand, in the two years she had worked with him, she had never once heard him boast of a conquest or relationship. Nor had he ever come on to her. His reputation had been built by others. Maybe his appeal lay in the mystery of what he was truly like.

He drained his styro cup of water. "And then, Gretch, Joe pulls this wild theory on her. Meself was so caught up in it I didn't see the holes. And she took it cool as a toad in a mineshaft. Never saw a lady like that one." He stopped beside her. "Did I explain Joe's hairy hypothesis?"

"In detail. Think he believes it?"

"Cannot tell, and I didn't yet ask him. He was quiet coming back—another of his thinking sprees—so I said nothing meself. I thought I'd see him this afternoon, but he trotted off doing something. He might. Then again he might be only baiting her."

"You didn't ask me, Tom, why I'm over here in Homicide, away from the protection of my ivory tower."

"I know already. Maynard Rust's feisty today and ye felt like slumming. Get away a bit."

Gretchen's mouth fell open. "How'd you know that?"

Tom refilled his styro cup. "Because, lass, I'm a detective and I takes me pleasure in detecting. I detect your fingers diddling thus, and ye only do that when you've been fighting with Maynard. One of your few nervous tics."

Gretchen found herself speechless, a condition rare to her. She stammered something on the order of, "Bet you say that to all the girls," but Tom's attention was diverted by the file clerk over at the window. She was calling to him and pointing to his desk and ringing phone. He bobbed across the room to answer it.

Was he simply such an observant person that he noticed her every mannerism? Or was he more interested in her than she realized? He had pegged the fight with Maynard correctly. That's exactly what happened, and exactly why she had to get out of that sterile lab awhile. Most people called Homicide the vultures' roost, but she loved it—the people in it—the hum of business being conducted. She should never have completed that second major in forensic chemistry. Now she'd never escape the lab. She wandered over to Tom's desk.

"Aye, Maude. No, if he says so, let's." Tom stared absently at Gretchen's nose. "Mm hm." He smiled at the voice on the other end. "Ye can still sign up for that honeymoon in Siberia, ye know." Pause. His face and ears flushed pink. "Later, Maude." He hung up.

"What honeymoon in Siberia?"

Tom leaned back. "The office password, currently. Anytime ye have a scheduling problem, a girlfriend problem, or no problem at all, ye plan your escape to a honeymoon in Siberia. Surprised it hasn't spread to the lab yet."

"Bunch of stuffy old crabs over there. They wouldn't even understand the ramifications of honeymooning in Siberia."

"Ah now, lass. Takes one to know one."

"Why you lousy bum! You're as bad as Joe—insult a poor defenseless girl at every opportunity."

Tom was riffling through the lap drawer of his desk. He pocketed a pen and small notebook and slammed it shut. "We're about to conduct an experiment. Ye may come along if ye care to. Hypnosis."

She followed him off toward the elevators "Wild horses couldn't keep me away—unless, of course, they happened to be in the immediate neighborhood."

Joe met them in the hallway of a wing Gretchen had never been in. He seemed grim, even preoccupied. He and Tommy glanced at each other and unspoken words passed between them.

All Tommy said was, "Again, eh?"

Joe nodded and shifted into a somewhat brighter mood. "I have it all lined up. She agrees, and Kramer's coming over in a few minutes. Hello, Gretch."

Gretchen nodded.

Tom frowned. "Her lawyer should be here too. Prevent problems later, mayhap."

"True, but she claimed the lawyer Persis is using is not only busy, but she doesn't think much of him. And she wouldn't know whom else to ask, so Kramer's bringing Harvey Spruce along."

Gretchen cut in. "Harvey's a defense counsel, right?"

"That's right." Joe led off down the long hall, so she fell in beside. "I remember Harvey saying once that he's a born-again Christian, so I called him. He's very much interested in the case because of the religious implications."

"A religious lawyer? Isn't that like a vegetarian shark?"

Tom shouldered Gretchen aside down another long hall. "A Christian Mescalero Apache defense lawyer. Only in Arizona."

They entered one of those conference rooms with molded plastic chairs, shiny plastic tabletop, plastic Venetian blinds and polyester draperies—a controlled plastic environment in which to make plastic decisions. Maynard had one just like it in his wing.

As they entered the door at the near end, Maude Drummond the jail matron was coming in the far end. Marie trotted along beside her. Even in her plain blue jail dress, Marie looked charmingly put together. Gretchen glanced quickly at Joe. He was sufficiently taken by the sight of Marie that he hesitated in mid-stride, then recommenced walking.

If Tom noticed, he was pretending not to. "Ah, Maude, me hearty, shall I tell Joe what ye said a few minutes ago?"

"You do and I'll break your arm. Sit here, please, Miss Kabrhan. You say Kramer's coming, Joe?"

"Should be here ten minutes ago. Do you have awhile, Maude? I'd like you to stay if you can."

"Sure. Should be interesting. I never saw one of these things work before."

Somehow Joe ended up sitting at Marie's side. Tom sat down opposite her.

Gretchen swung around the table to settle in close beside Tom. "I hate to pick up a book and start reading on page 86. Anyone care to fill me in on the other 85?"

Joe smiled. "There are certain details of the initial incident—the car bomb—that no one can remember. Marie has agreed to undergo hypnosis as a means of recalling them."

Gretchen looked at Marie. "Why? What if the answers turn out to be wrong? Hurtful? Know what I mean?"

Marie nodded. "I didn't like the idea at first, for that reason. But then I thought about it awhile and decided to put out a fleece. Ever put out a fleece? It's based on the story of Gideon in Judges. You ask God to provide some sign to assure you He wants you to do something—or make a particular choice."

"Fine." Gretchen let it go. "What was your fleece?"

"That Persis would call within five minutes. She did, for no particular reason. So I figured God's light was green. Besides, there are all sorts of things Persis and I can't exactly remember about that time. It was a horrible, confusing, foggy blur, the whole day. This could be very helpful. I want to know too." She looked sideways at Joe. He was supposed to be the enemy—the other side in this cops-and-robbers game—but you'd never know it from her.

"Besides," Joe added, "this is nonstipulated."

Gretchen frowned. "You mean, like a lie detector test is nonstipulated? You can't use it in court?"

"Right."

Harvey and Kramer were late by fifteen minutes, as it turned out. Dr. Kramer, one of three psychiatrists the department used from time to time, looked more like a football coach, replete with bull neck, six-six frame, blond burr cut and a scar across his cheek.

Harvey Spruce was just as square and stocky, but he stood a foot shorter. The sun crinkles in his brown face had softened with age into a network of jovial laugh-lines.

After introductions, he plunked down beside Joe. "Sorry we're late. Got talking about the Ringgardner thing. Any news?"

"Not till next week. Marie, Harvey Spruce here is your legal representative in this matter; we thought you should have one."

She nodded. She looked a bit swamped in this sea

of faces. Hers was an innocent, vulnerable sort of look, and Gretchen could not imagine her plying her former trade.

Dr. Kramer displaced Tom to sit across from Marie, bumping Gretchen down a chair. His voice rumbled like a baritone brook, smooth, gentle, avuncular. Gretchen knew he'd put scores of witnesses under like this, although she'd never seen it done. Hypnotic trances always seemed so phony to her. Then again, she'd never watched a real one up close. She concentrated on Marie, observing the girl's facial muscles, her eyes, her hands.

Marie went casually, quietly away. Her features relaxed. Gretchen sat amazed, watching total oblivion come to the girl's face. She glanced around. Everyone present seemed spellbound by Dr. Kramer's smooth style—everyone but Joe. His attention was on Marie, his face tight with worry. He couldn't be concerned for her health and safety. Did he anticipate damaging evidence that Gretchen couldn't foresee?

Joe passed a handwritten page to Kramer. The doctor laid his finger on the first line. "Miss Kabrhan, you, Persis, and Cat are driving through Phoenix. You're in town for the first time. You just left the freeway at Indian School and now you're driving east toward your motel. What color is the car you're riding in?"

"Blue."

"What shade of blue?"

"Light blue. Sort of baby blue."

"Who's driving?"

"I am."

"Do you mind driving like this?"

"Heavy traffic. I don't like heavy traffic."

"Here's your motel. You pull in. Now what?"

"Cat's taking a long time signing us in. The car is real hot inside. I'm not sure I like Phoenix. It's so hot. Here comes Cat with the key."

"Where are you going to park? Right in front of your room?"

"Can't. There's no room. There's our door over there, number eight. The closest slot is out in the lot here. That's close enough."

"Can the three of you handle everything all right?"

"We'll make two trips."

"What's happening?"

"Cat's taking the two big suitcases. Persis has her file box and briefcase. And the coffee maker."

"What are you carrying?"

"The two typewriters. I wish Cat would get one of those little electronic things that don't weigh anything. The daisy wheel's not so bad, but I'm tired of lugging this monster around."

Kramer looked at Joe and abandoned the notes. "Miss Kabrhan, what else do you dislike about Cat?"

"Oh, you know. She's so cold. And she makes the coffee too strong. I can't even drink it. She complains all the time that I don't get things done. She shouldn't be so bossy. I don't work for her."

"Is it true you dislike her intensely? Maybe even hate her?"

"No. She just bugs me, is all."

"You've brought in all the bags and things. Who

goes out to the car next?"

"Persis. I think she's going after the travelers' checks. They're in the glove compartment. But she's coming back in and she doesn't have them. I don't know why she went out."

Joe flashed a hasty series of signs across to Kramer, and drew a curved line under his arm. Gretchen had no idea they were fluent in sign language, either of them.

"What's this?" Kramer glanced at the notes. "Persis' dress is torn under the sleeve. What does she say about that?"

" 'Marie, I'm just going to have to quit impersonating windmills. Look at this. It happens every time I get wound up. Did you bring in the mending kit?' "

"And you reply. . . ?"

"It's here somewhere. The little zipper pocket, I think. Here it is. I'll fix it for you."

Kramer waited a long moment and then prompted, "Go on."

" 'Would you, dear? This is the dress I should wear. I understand the sponsoring church is ultra-conservative. If I wear the flowered number, a third of the congregation will turn purple and another third will die laughing. We wouldn't want anyone to die. Where's Cat? There you are. Did Jules leave word?' "

"Keep going," Kramer cooed. "What next?"

" 'Not yet. Wonder what set him off this time.' "

" 'He has been moodier than usual lately, hasn't he?' "

" 'Marie, what did the gas gauge say when we

pulled in?' "

"Who's saying that?" Kramer interrupted.

"Cat. What business is it of hers, anyway? She didn't do any driving."

"And your reply?" Kramer asked.

"About a quarter tank, I think."

" 'Better fill it up before we go. Then we won't have to mess around looking for gas at odd hours.'

"You'll just have to wait a minute. I'm only half done here."

Silence. Gretchen could hear Tom breathing beside her, it was so quiet.

Kramer let the silence ride a few moments, then prodded gently. "You're still working on the torn sleeve. Isn't it going right?"

"No. It's so slow. This stupid fabric puckers if you don't take real tiny stitches. I'm not even listening to them, really."

"But your ears and mind hear. Tell me what each person is saying as you work."

"Cat says, 'Persis, do you want the briefcase, or just the folder?'

"Persis says, 'The folder's enough.'

" 'Marie, aren't you done yet?' "

"That's Cat?" Kramer asked.

"That's Cat. She's always so impatient. She drives me right up the wall. Persis says, 'I saw an el cheap-o gas station beyond the motel on the right, Cat. Perhaps you can fill it up, since Marie's busy.'

"Cat says, 'She says she'll be done in a minute.' " Marie's voice purred along without tone or inflection. "Persis says, 'Cat, I'd rather you go do it, please.' "

GUN-RUNNING WIMP

Joe perched on a tall stool, the better to watch over Henrietta Nieswonger's shoulder. She played her terminal as a harpist plays in a symphony orchestra, her fingers stroking in rapid staccato. The printer beside her chattered crossly and spat forth its readout line on line.

```
PAGE 01
TO: AVD2        FROM ALETS
IH
RE: W1091102 NAM/BARBRIE, HENRY J
SEARCH ON LAST-NAME, FIRST-NAME, SEX
     PLUS MI-DOB-RAC-HGT-HAI-EYE REVEALS
NO HIT - AUTOMATED SYSTEM

PAGE O1
TO: AVD2       FROM: ALETS
```

```
IN
LI BARBRIE HENRY J
NO RECORD FOR CRITERIA GIVEN
ANI END

PAGE 01
TO: AVD2     FROM: ALETS
IW
W1091102 RE: BARBRIE HENRY J SEX/M
NO WANTS
CHECKING NCIC
IJ
IL01
7
W1091102
NO NCIC WANT DOB/102463 NAM/BARBRIE,
HENRY J SEX/M RAC/W
```

Henrietta ripped off the readout and handed it to him. "Satisfied?"

"Guess so."

"Whaddaya mean, 'Guess so'? You sound like my second husband. You should be disappointed?"

"Everyone else in her organization seems to have such a colorful past, it's a shame he's so lackluster."

Henny sat back and let him light her cigarette for her. "My youngest son's taking this folk music course at ASU. Fluff stuff. Goes around the house all day singing, 'High Barbaree.' Ever hear 'High Barbaree'?"

"Don't think so."

She shrugged. "Sorta like this fellow's name."

A little bell went ding inside Joe's head. "We haven't been checking variations. Henny, try NC on some other spellings—D-E-B-A-R-B-A-R-I-E, that kind of thing."

She laid her cigarette aside and poked at her keyboard. "Whadya say the J is?"

"John."

"That's right." She hummed to herself. The machine stuttered and beeped. She sat back. "Tied up. Be a minute. Wanna play a few hands of poker or something?"

"Naw. I hate losing."

"Chicken." She grinned and took a drag on her cigarette.

Joe slid off his stool and wandered over to the window. Like a disjointed caterpillar, the traffic in the street below lurched and paused. A young woman hastened along the far sidewalk. In height and build she was a match for Marie.

Marie. Minutes later he realized he was still daydreaming about her.

"Bingo! Maybe." Henny studied her display as pale green paper jerked out of the printer.

PAGE 01
RO AVD2   FROM NCIC
ID
IL01   CA
DL/NO: R0714223 + B/D:10-24-63 +
NAME:DEBARBARIE HENRY JOHN +
ADDR AS OF 12-05-87:1774 OLEANDER PL BIG SUR CA 93920

IDENTIFYING INFORMATION:

SEX:MALE + HT:5-4 + WT148 + EYES:BN +
HAIR:BN + PTH/ADDR AS OF 06-02-85:
US NAV FAC PT SUR BIG SUR CA 93920
DEPARTMENTAL ACTIONS:
NONE
CONVICTIONS:
VIOL/DT CONV/DT SEC/VIOL DKT/NO FINE
DISP COURT VEH/LIC
03-17-88 05-24-88 22153ABCFR 05504 500 B
FC19143 TNC188
FAILURES TO APPEAR:
NONE
END

"That's our boy. Gained a little weight since then." Joe studied it twice over. "Run a license check, huh? California TNC188. And what's a 22153AB code of federal regulations?"

"That's what I just asked the brain here." She leaned forward to squint at the screen. Her eyebrows shot up. "Seems your lackluster Mr. Barbrie was convicted of transporting explosives across a state line. The B means without a valid permit."

"Oh, yeah?" Joe leaned in close over her shoulder.

The machine made triumphant little beeping noises. Henny punched it again. Joe had no idea how she knew when and where to hit keys.

"The vehicle was registered to Henry DeBarbarie and apparently junked. No registration or transfer beyond December of '88."

"Moved to another state?"

"It'd show up. You mean like from California to Wisconsin."

"You have the court and docket numbers there. Can you dig me out the case records? I want to know if the explosives were plastiques and if they nailed him on any additional charges in California. Also if he's ever been linked up to any bomb operations."

"You want the moon, hotshot. Don't you ever do any investigating on your own?"

"Not when I can get some gorgeous chick to do it for me."

"You are referring, of course, to the computer. Well, gorgeous, let's get this over with." She re-arranged herself in her chair and went to work.

Joe started back toward the window and stopped halfway. "Point Sur Naval Facility. He probably worked there. Can you do a military check on him too?"

"Why not? I get paid by the hour. Bet he worked on the base and got caught filching torpedoes. Now what does a mild-mannered little twerp like that want with a torpedo?"

"Could be firecrackers from the PX too. 'Explosives' takes in anything from the H bomb to Tommy's cigarettes."

Henny's nose wrinkled. "He hasn't changed brands yet? That Irishman has beef jerky where his tongue oughta be. Here's your military record. He's never been in the armed farces."

"Forces, Henny. Forces."

"My oldest son spent two years in the army.

Farces. Trust me." She sat back and watched her machine purr.

It was over an hour before Joe finally got out of there.

"So what do you think of our Mr. Barbrie?" Joe watched his partner's eyebrows move about at random across his face. Tom had expressive brows anyway, and when he was thinking—in this case, reading between the lines of Henrietta's printout— his eyebrows were constantly lifting in surprise, arching in doubt, crowding together in thought.

"Me opinion of this stark and mechanical read-out: the boy went to work on the base as a civvie. Being a simple, trusting soul, he fell in with black marketeers, or possibly gunrunners. Made deliveries of explosives and might not even be knowing what he was carrying. He made enough money to move into fancier digs in December, was caught with the goods a couple months later. Tried in federal court because he's a civilian, fined and turned loose because of no priors. Left the Golden State for the Land of 10,000 Lakes soon after."

"That's what I got too. Haven't asked him yet, though."

Tom laid the papers aside and took another bite of his Extraburger. "Now meself is thinking, having talked to this Barbrie at length, that he's not got the facilities upstairs to be a successful bomber. Nor a shootist. He's not stupid, mind ye, as evidenced by the way he's mastered the Bible. But neither is he the conniving sort, able to plan a crime in detail."

"Putting on an act? Following someone else's

game plan?"

Tom sipped his cola. It slurped. He scowled at the cup and swirled the ice about, no doubt hoping more cola would drop to the bottom. "Nay, Jose. In certain ways he's limited. Naive. Perfect patsy for munitions runners using a naval base as their source of supply."

"Brother Jennings said he knows munitions and explosives."

"Aye. I'm basing me judgment upon the impression I got of him. I doubt it signifies."

"How about perfect patsy for a bomber? He scrapes up the raw materials and either throws them or wires them, but someone else is responsible. I vote for sure that he's capable of blind devotion. A sheep to follow meekly behind a shepherd."

Tom munched thoughtfully on his dinner awhile. Joe had already finished his. Some supper. Burger and fries at a fast-food joint. He missed his kids. He wished he had a nice home to put them in, a woman to love them and him, to feed them and him right, to welcome him into bed with soft hands and a warm heart. The thought of Marie popped into his head so unexpectedly it startled him. Why should he associate her with a warm and happy home? She was soiled. Tainted. And charmingly appealing.

"Me opinion of Henry Barbrie, Joe, is that he's not our man. First, he's not had access to explosives at Point Sur for a long time. I was guessing he's essentially innocent in his dealings there, and the federal court seems to share that guess. But if we're wrong, second, he had to learn a lot about outside sources for explosives whilst romping with his black-market friends. And if the navy were the friends' source, there'd be no need to discuss any others. Ye see me meaning?"

"His associates wouldn't be giving him one little datum more information than he had to know."

"Precisely. Then there's third, that he himself was running guns or selling military playthings or whatever. An independent businessman without other operatives."

"That would take quite a bit of schmarts, not to mention chutzpah."

"Neither of which Henry has in abundance. Aye, he's a possibility, as are they all. But meself would look elsewhere first." Tom finished off his hamburger and wiped his mouth. "You're staring off into space like a drugged sphynx. Be ye solving our crime here, or just daydreaming?"

Joe sighed and rubbed his face with both hands. "I'm getting old, Tommy. My brain keeps slipping gears."

"That's not age, that's just your transmission. Marie keeps getting in the way of your serious cogitations, eh?"

Joe gaped and hastily put his face back together. "You're a leprechaun, Tommy, able to see right through mortal men."

"If ye wish. A leprechaun with an overactive thyroid, which explains me extreme height as leprechauns go." Tom leaned foward. "Joe, ye need a woman. You're a family man skin to marrow. Ye deserve the best, and you'll do no better than Marie Kabrhan."

"She's a prostitute."

"Your wife was an adulteress, but ye forgave her. You're still forgiving of her, to cling to her memory all these years. Can ye not see? Marie considers herself forgiven by God Himself and I believe it. These folks say so, and 'tis their line of expertise. The only holdout's yourself. And I dare say Marie's attitude is more deserving of forgiveness than was your wife's."

Joe felt his neck turning red. Partner or no, Tom had no right to say something like that about Louise. He never even met her.

Tom kept talking. "Come to grips with this Marie thing—resolve it once for all—and then your aging brain will cease slipping gears."

"She may well be a murderer."

"Possibly. So set yourself up a conditional plan of action. If she be guilty, why then quit her. But if it happens she's innocent, why then you'll do such-and-so."

"What such-and-so, specifically?"

Tom started gathering the debris of supper onto the tray. "Jose, me brawny lad, if Marie looked at me the way she looks at you, meself'd be courting her this very minute."

"Oh, come on, Tommy! Get off it."

"She's in love." Tom cast him a sidewise glance. "As is yourself."

Why did Joe feel so angry? He burned. "Gonna call the kids. Be back in a minute."

He walked out to the pay phone in the foyer, jammed his quarter in and punched in the numbers without thinking. Marie in love? Bull. Himself in love? Double bull.

"Sanchez residence, Gloria speaking."

"Hola, sugar. How's it going?"

"You going to be done with your work, soon, Daddy? Aunt Fel says I have to get my shots Friday. I want you to take me."

"I'll see what I can do. You and Rico getting ready for bed?"

"Rico's finishing his homework. Daddy, Miss Kabrhan is such a nice lady. Are you going to marry her?"

"Not that I know of. Did Tommy tell you to say that?"

"No. Rico and I were talking about her. She likes kids, we can tell. She'd be such a good mommy. She wouldn't ever leave us all alone, I bet."

The same old knife stabbed his heart all over again. He fondly liked to think that Glo was too young to have been affected by her mother's negligence. . . . that if he were a good enough father, Fel would be all the mother his kids needed. Fat chance.

If he really wanted to, he could find a dozen women who'd be a better mother than Marie . . . who gave her baby up for adoption. That told you what kind of mother she was. . . . The kind of confused, too young, unwed mother who would sacrifice her own needs as a mother for the ultimate welfare of her child.

Every time he came up with what was wrong with her, his own mind negated his objections. He couldn't even trust his own heart. But then he never could do that, not safely.

"Daddy? Why aren't you talking?"

"Guess I don't have anything to say. I just wanted to call."

"Rico wants to know what's 426 divided by 71."

"Six."

She turned away from the receiver but her piercing soprano still rattled his eardrum as she gave Rico the answer. "He wants to know how you got that."

"I asked myself how many times 7 goes into 42. Hey, Tommy's waiting. I have to go. Good night, sugar. And say good night to Einstein for me there."

"Good night, Daddy. Remember about the shots Friday, okay?"

"Okay." He hung it up and cursed fate that he couldn't be snuggled up with his kids now, reading Glo a bedtime story, helping Rico with his arithmetic.

Marie. He hungered for her. Why fool himself with all his high-minded, pious objections? She was a hooker who quit, she was a charmer who had won over Tommy and the kids with little more than a few words and a smile; she was a beautiful young woman, freckles and all.

Through the glass inner doors he watched Tom wad the readouts together into a clumsy fold and stuff them into his pocket. He tipped his paper and styro into the waste receptacle and tossed the tray on top of it. Tommy understood people. Tommy understood Joe better than Joe did. And Tommy advised courting Marie.

As Tom pushed out the inner door, Joe turned to fall in beside him. "The zoo's open tonight—one of their moonlight specials. Drop me off there, all right?"

Tom held the outside door for him. "Me pleasure. Call me in a couple hours. I'll be at the office. Meantime I'll talk to Henry and make sure our suppositions be correct. If I should need ye in an emergency, where might the zoo people come looking for ye?"

"Great Indian Hornbill is as good a spot as any. Quiet there, few visitors, no nearby lights. Good place to think."

Air conditioning is nice, to a point, but Joe liked the warm and heavy air of night much better than the phony chill inside the Extraburger. He crawled into Rocinante and cranked the window down as far as it would go. He let the night air blow on his face. It did nothing toward blowing away the cobwebs in his mind. It cooled, but it did not purify.

TO SET A TRAP

A minor mountain of paperwork sulked on her desk, and Gretchen sulked right back at it. Maynard wanted this pile cleared yesterday. He complained in no uncertain terms when she got around to cross-filing Joe and Tom's car bomb before Hugh Bartoli's strangling. She used the argument that the Magen case was high profile and they had to stay on top of it, whereas Hugh's victim had been a homeless druggie. She didn't believe the argument any more than Maynard did. She just felt like doing Tom's, that was all. So all Hugh's photos and prelims were just lying there waiting.

Let 'em wait. She stood, turned her back on the whole mess and headed for the elevators. She was tired of doing Maynard's paperwork. Surely someone else in this lavishly populated department could assemble case files. Let Maynard file Hugh's material, if he was so hot to see it done. In fact, a lot of things Maynard did — and did not do — irritated her lately.

The elevator hummed and jerked. Why was she coming over here, anyway? She had no pressing business in Homicide. She was strolling the halls daydreaming, knowing exactly where she was going and pretending she didn't. What might it be like to have Joe Rodriguez as a boyfriend rather than Maynard Rust? In the first place, it would never happen. Joe paired up with some girl now and then casually, but never, so far as she knew, to the point of getting really serious. Apparently the only way to snag Joe Rodriguez was to marry him, and he didn't seem to be in a marrying mood.

Gretchen Rodriguez? Hardly! Who wants the same partner for a whole lifetime, and that's what you'd be stuck with. On the other hand, no cheating. You could depend on Joe for that. Once yours, he'd be exclusively yours — prudish, laid back, gentle, considerate, a bit dull. Gretchen longed for the peace and security of a relationship like that.

How about Gretchen Flaherty? She almost laughed out loud. If a man wasn't married by thirty-one — she knew how old Tommy was because she looked him up in personnel — he wasn't going to marry. But then, in her mid-twenties, neither was she. She thought about Tom's boundless energy, his constant motion. She longed for a vital relationship even more than for peace and security.

She entered the squad room and paused. Joe was sitting at his desk with his legs sprawled out, as per usual. Tom lay across Joe's desk, propped with one elbow like a Roman reclining at dinner. They were arguing, it appeared, very quietly. Should she interrupt? She hesitated, but only for a moment.

"Hi, guys. Am I interrupting?"

"Aye, and welcome." Tom squirmed around to sitting. "Joe spent last evening communing with the hornbill at the zoo, one of his thinking marathons. We believe we know who our bomber is, and we're planning a surprise."

"Gloriosky! Just like on the TV! I've heard about your traps, Joe—a legend in your own time. Can I help?" Gretchen felt an electric little tingle, an excitement transmitted from these two. She perched on a corner of Joe's desk. "Hey, I'm serious. I want to help out."

Joe was staring at her, his lips a thin white line. "Tommy, there's our pipeline to Persis."

"Aye, the very thing."

Joe shook his head. "But not at the zoo. Stage it somewhere else. Papago Golf Course maybe, or the ice rink at Tower Plaza. Better, the botanical garden, way at the back near the display hall. Or the lath house."

"Joe, me lad, the zoo's perfect. First off, ye can ..."

"Too many kids. No. If some little kid got hurt ..."

"School's in session. No kids, except school groups. Them we can avoid outright or shunt off elsewhere." Tom leaned forward earnestly. "Look, Joe, ye know every inch of that place—back alleys, behind the cages, the layout, the shortcuts, where the alligators be hiding. 'Tis your turf. And we can cover ye six different ways there."

Joe looked grim. "So many variables on this one. No solid evidence. Just a whole basketful of circumstances. I'm guessing, Tommy, that's all. What if I'm wrong? What if the killer's someone else and strikes from some direction we didn't anticipate?"

"We'll anticipate all the directions. But you're not wrong. Ye picked this one right out of the hat, I'm certain."

"Picked who?" The tingle was becoming lightning. Gretchen glanced around nervously and lowered her voice. "Who is it?"

"A pure guess, Gretch." Joe wagged his head. "You really want in?"

"Really!"

"Then I want you to be on the lookout for anything and everything, not just one possibility. If I'm right, hot diggity. But if I'm wrong, I don't want any of us so locked into one prospect that we miss the real culprit. Or worse, let an accident happen."

Tommy added, "Ye see, Gretchen, so long as Marie be comfortably ensconced in our municipal slammer, nothing's going to happen."

"So you think she's really it."

"You're jumping too fast, lass. Mark this—if she's the one, she can't do anything in there. But if she be the target, the killer can't reach her."

Gretchen picked it up. "And if the killer wants to pin the whole thing on her, he can't unless she's free to kill again, so to speak. But she confessed, and it looked good."

Joe nodded. "To get Persis out from under bond. In fact, Persis leaves Phoenix this evening on a 7:30

flight; so if we want all the principals in town, we don't have much time left."

"I got the impression they'd be driving to Riverside."

"Jules is keeping the car here a couple days, he and Henry." Joe rubbed his eyes. "They have a real mess to clean up, I guess; Cat was the power behind the throne and Marie carried a lot of weight too. With both gone, the system is all fouled up—the other subordinates running in circles, local pastors trying to lend a hand and getting things fouled up worse . . . Persis would've been out of here already, if she didn't have to iron out so many wrinkles. Churches needing this and that."

"Mmm." Gretchen tried to think; things were flying by her too fast. "Joe, what if Marie's confession is genuine? Remember you were telling how Jules was boasting about putting his claws into Persis? And he probably wasn't? What if it was Marie? What if she was the one who was afraid Cat would squeal? Maybe make her lose her job? Something else? Considering the background on both those women, there are a dozen things they could be holding over each other's head."

"If it is, the idea won't work. Might not anyway." Joe looked strained. Was it just the case?

Gretchen leaned toward him a little. "Joe? What else is bothering you?"

He looked at her and almost spoke, but he closed his mouth again.

Tommy grimaced. "Jerry's off on another toot; push Joe up or out. We need this one, lass."

"To impress upon the powers that be that they

can't afford to dump him. I see." Gretchen clapped her hands. "Okay, fellas, let's all make a miracle here. Catch that perp!"

Tom hopped off the desk. "The lieutenant's already made arrangements with the commish. We spring Marie, and let everyone know she's free as a bird—available for target practice, framing, what have ye."

"Heady stuff. And dangerous."

Joe nodded. "That's why I hate to use the zoo."

"I agree with Tommy. You want someplace where the killer will feel free to move—someplace urban and public. Assassins fit a certain environmental pattern and the zoo is just fine for that. The botanical garden is not. And like he says, if you have a turf in Maricopa County, the zoo is it."

She wondered why Joe should be so hesitant, so grim and worried. He had pulled this sort of coup before—accurately determining a killer's identity and then revealing him in the act by setting up a sometimes elaborate, always meticulous trap. He gained three convictions out of three attempts that way, and in all cases had successfully skated clear of any countercharges of police entrapment. He should be confident, unless...

Marie. He was afraid to expose Marie. Warm, cute, vulnerable Marie. How much of his feeling was strictly paternal and protective, and how much ran deeper? And why was he so certain her confession was false? Was he simply fooling himself?

Joe sat up straight and scooted his chair forward. "Gretch, I doubt Persis and her crew know much about the internal workings of the department—the day-to-day. Especially your end in the lab. Call Persis and tell her you need her to sign something—some obscure form. You think of a reason. Run over to the motel and get it, and while you're there, strike up a conversation. We'll tell you what we want her to know."

"Right. Hey, I love this cloak-and-dagger stuff! Will my trench coat be department issue?"

Tom snorted. "This time of year? You'd melt. Have ye a gun?"

"Sure."

"That works?"

"Whaddaya mean by that? Is that some sexist remark?"

Tom grinned like a ten-year-old. "Two weeks ago we used that little Lori out of traffic detail. Ye ever meet her? She hauls out her two-inch from her purse, ye see, and it be so gummed up with purse lint and melted lipstick and who knows what that she couldn't so much as budge the cylinder. If ye think *she* was embarrassed, ye should have seen her sergeant."

"I qualified this quarter with my two-inch. And with my four-inch I can shoot the fleas off a squirrel's tail." Gretchen was so excited she couldn't sit still. Flush Maynard Rust and his lousy paperwork! After five years on the force she was finally getting to see some action. Some real action!

"All right, Gretch, this is what you let slip to Persis . . ."

Marie paused in the dressing room doorway.

"This way, Miss Kabrhan."

Most of the matrons Marie had crossed paths with in her time looked like weight lifters. This Maude Drummond was hefty, but at least she was fairly well built. She was polite too, even respectful. Marie appreciated that. Obediently she started down the long hallway beside the matron. Here was another sign she really was being freed; normally you weren't allowed to walk beside.

It was good to be out of the county's version of high fashion and into her own clothes again. But why? Was her release even real? Marie felt a double sensation of confusion and delight as the final door opened and she stepped out into the booking room.

The delight soared instantly. Joe Rodriguez and Tom Flaherty stood over by the main desk. Tom and the clerk were laughing. Joe saw her immediately—obviously he had been watching for her. She felt herself grinning irrepressibly. She tried to rearrange her face into a more sophisticated expression, a mein of nonchalance, and her face resisted successfully. Joe was smiling too. Had his heart changed at all? The matron stopped. Marie kept walking.

Tom scrawled his name across the bottom of a triplicate form and grinned at her. "Glad ye could make it to your coming-out party, lass."

"Not as glad as I am. I don't get this. Not any of it."

Joe piloted her by an elbow toward the big glass doors. They swung away, letting the Arizona heat hit her full face. Freedom. "Your confession had too many holes in it. Nice try, though."

"Oh? Name one."

"You know them better than I do. At any rate, you're out. The commissioner signed the paperwork. Shall . . ."

"Does Persis know?"

Tom fell in beside them. "She's on 'er way to Riverside by now, near as we know. Call her tonight, I suggest."

"Oh, good! Then she made it. Praise the Lord!" She felt like a schoolgirl, a silly little schoolgirl. She could practically feel herself glowing and not only could she do nothing about it, she didn't care. She felt Joe's presence at her left. Tom was just as close on her right, but she didn't feel him. Not the same way.

"Well, I'll be hying meself back to the salt mine. Delighted, Marie." Tom nodded and parted company, angling off up the street. Was that Rocinante he was headed for? She tried to remember the license number and could not.

Joe opened the right-hand door of a bright-green beetle. She plopped into the seat without hesitation. He slid in the other side and his door clunked shut. He stared awhile at the Wolfsburg emblem on the steering column. She sat silent, in no hurry. Apparently resigned to whatever, he twisted the ignition key. The bug coughed, groaned, and purred in that order. He watched the sideview mirror for a break in traffic.

She ought to say something. "Is this Tom's car."

"What tipped you off?"

"The paint job. How many kelly green beetles are there? Is Tom as close to his car as you are to yours?"

"Naw. Every now and then I steal it from him and change the oil, do the plugs and points. If it was up to him, it'd never get serviced. I like dinking around with cars and he couldn't care less." Joe had to floor it to slip into the street. The points and oil might be up to snuff, but the little car still had the pickup of a fifteen-year-old basset hound.

"What does Tom like dinking around with? Horses? Irishmen and horses go together."

"He doesn't care beans about anything that moves. His passion is real estate. Sinks all his pennies into land."

"He'll die wealthy."

"The Howard Hughes of Phoenix Homicide. Economy here is depressed, but that won't last. Soon as it turns around..."

Silence.

A thousand questions clamored in her mind. Perhaps now that Persis was safely on her way, Marie could venture to ask a few of them. She would start with something innocuous and work up to the tantalizing ones. "Where are we going, may I ask?"

"Thought we might go see the orangutan exhibit at the zoo. It's one of the world's best. Celebrate your release with a zebra cola. Sound okay?"

"Great. On that picnic, I didn't get to see much of the zoo itself at all." She hesitated. "Tom told me once how much you like to take your children to the zoo. I'm honored." She paused again, uncertain. "He told me about your wife too."

"Tom talks a lot."

"But not too much. I'm glad you didn't say he talks too much, because it's not true. You know, it's so sad when you love someone very much and they don't bother to return your love."

"I never thought of it quite that way before, but you're right."

"It's the same with God, you know. He loves you fully and completely and you're either ignoring Him or refusing His gifts for you. Unrequited love."

The turn signal ticked quietly. Joe pulled out onto Van Buren Street and fell in behind an empty cattle truck. She was no lawyer, but she'd picked up a few points of law here and there. She mulled them over. No matter how she sorted things out, the conclusion was the same.

"Joe? We really going to the zoo?"

"Mmm hmm."

"Now let's see. I'm booked for murder one. Suddenly the matron trots me off to the showers and hands me my own clothes. Here's the sealed plastic bag with my purse and everything. Now since I wasn't bailed out..."

"Bail is standard practice, including murder one."

"By richer people than any of my friends are. As I was saying, here I am walking free, a confessed murderer. No bail bond, no hearing, in the company of a cop yet—a homicide investigator. To the zoo, for Pete's sake. So I'm bait, right? Cheese in a mousetrap."

Joe's head snapped around. He stared at her so intently he almost drifted out of his lane. That was why he seemed so grim.

"Who is it, Joe? Who killed Cat?"

"We don't know. It's a guess—pure surmise with

nothing solid behind it. We're hoping this will flush the killer. You're sharper than I gave you credit for, Marie."

"Thank you."

He chewed his lip awhile. "Look, Marie. I'm sorry. Tom and I both are, but we can't see any other way."

"I'm not objecting . . ."

"We think you might be the target. As long as you're in jail, you're safe. But you won't be there forever; we don't have enough to make the charge stick. A good defense lawyer could tear your confession to shreds. In fact, Harvey already did. When you're vulnerable and the killer tries again, you'll be unprotected. Tom and I argued this scam a long time."

"So you're going to lure the killer into trying for me while you have me covered. Protected."

"Exactly. I hate to use you. At least this way you'll have half a dozen cops around."

"You're sure he'll try?"

He nodded. "Pretty sure. We spread the word to everyone involved, by one means or another—Tom to Jules and Henry and some of the other people in your outfit, Gretch to Persis. They all heard you're scared. You were told to stay in Arizona but you're gonna split as soon as you can, leave Persis' operation, disappear. So this will be the killer's last good chance to reach you. Lucky for the killer that I think you're cute and decided to date you this afternoon. I probably have ulterior motives."

"There's a pun on zoos and monkeyshines here, but I'm not going to touch it."

Joe chuckled grimly.

"So the killer knows I'm at the zoo. He. Jules?"

"You said *he.* I didn't."

She stared at him openmouthed. "Persis? No, Joe! Not her."

"I told you before; pure guess. Could be anyone. A total stranger." He changed lanes. The bug paused at a light, the gearshift trembling.

"Joe? What if something goes wrong?"

"That's what I hate about using you in this scam."

"I don't mean me. I mean you. Do you realize what will happen if I'm really the target and the killer succeeds? Nothing, Joe. That's what. I already have eternal life. The killer kills my body, but he can't touch *me.* If he gets you, you're dead. And he just might—you'll be right in the thick of it. You might be dead in an hour. Then what?"

"My kids are orphans. Don't think I haven't thought about *that* a million times."

"Stop it. You know what I'm talking about. Eternally dead. In hell forever because you refused Jesus."

"Marie, now don't start that . . ." He closed his mouth and opened it again. "I'm straight. I keep my nose clean."

"Maybe now, but not always. You can't claim a totally clean life. Nobody can. You know that one black mark is all it takes, and sinful thoughts are black marks just the same as sinful deeds."

"Get off the religion, okay?" His knuckles on the steering wheel were white, his face so tight it was almost red. She had struck home. In what way?

They rode in silence. She saw the zoo sign up ahead, a big billboard with a sleepy-eyed rhino peeking over. They swung into the left turn lane, paused, waited. The light changed. The bug lurched around the corner into the drive across the desert of Papago Park, but Joe didn't continue past the green sign that promised zoo parking up ahead. He flicked the flasher on and pulled over the roadside. The tires whispered to a halt in the coarse dry gravel.

She started to lay a hand on his arm and restrained herself. She wanted so much to reach out to him, but she thought better of it. She waited, watching, twisted in the seat toward him.

He stared straight ahead at the past, his arms draped over the wheel. "Louise. My wife, Louise. Tom told you Louise was slipping around with this university professor. Wavy-haired, tall, favored pinstripe suits. Psych department at ASU. They were a twosome for a couple of months before I found out. I thought that kind of thing was all over with her. She promised. I thought she was playing me straight. Then this second guy. I blew up. It's usually not like me, but all those months I thought she was being a good girl. . . ."

The flashers clicked rhythmically. Should she speak? She held her peace and waited.

"I can't remember what I said to her exactly, except that I really blew up. And she was shrieking just as loud, as if it was all my fault she was cheating. I told her she ought to be dead. Told her to go to hell. I told her to go to hell and then I left. She left too—left the kids alone, and one of them in diapers yet—and took off with her friend. Four hours later Monty's unit was dragging her and her pal both out of the canal. Drowned. Right after I told her . . ." He stopped, licked his lips. "Told her where to go."

"You once accused me of letting thoughts fester. You've never mentioned this to anyone since then? Not even to Tom?"

"Not even to Tom."

"I can sympathize with your feelings of guilt and frustration. I guess 'emphathize' is more the word. Murderous thoughts as well as sinful deeds."

"Murderous thoughts. Nicely put."

"I'm sure by now you've convinced yourself that you can't literally consign someone to hell, no matter how mad you get."

He smiled bitterly. "All rationalized away. Except it won't go away. Not in all these years."

"You know what Persis would be telling you right now. It can be forgiven. It's not just a theory, either. It works."

"Cosmic eraser. That blood message she wrote out." He turned to look at her, to read her face. What did he see? She wanted him to see love and concern, but did he?

She wasn't the preacher Persis was, not the orator. She wanted to choose a few perfect words to drive home the message of God's love, of God's cleansing. She yearned to explain how remorse is useless unless it leads to repentance and commitment to Jesus. She had watched hundreds of people give up fighting God and throw themselves on His mercy. She had watched them walk away cleansed and whole—new people. How much happier he would be if he could surrender all to Jesus. But the words fled, leaving her tongue a shambles. She could only stammer, "Jesus loves you. And I do too."

TIGER, TIGER, BURNING BRIGHT

Gretchen slid into the passenger side and slammed the door. "Is this the fabled Rocinante?" She slammed the door three times more before the latch would hold. "Yep. Sure is."

"Nobody's perfect." Tom grinned and pulled out into traffic.

She looked him over — the fancy cowboy boots, the checkered shirt, the stiff jeans. "Nice hat, Tom. Fifteen gallons if it's a pint."

"Irish cowboy. The very best kind. Ye know, I'm sure, that all those cowboy songs ye grew up with are transplanted Irish ballads. 'As I was a-walking one morning for pleasure, I spied a cowpuncher come riding along . . .' Pure Irish."

"Terrible cultural mishmash."

"And yourself, looking so bright and perky. May I compliment your lovely dress? I like flowered prints."

"Why thank you. I save this dress for special oc-
casions—presidential inaugurations, coronations,
market openings, payday, the afternoon off. You
know."

"So Maynard gave ye the afternoon off, did he?"

"Hardly." She laughed. "He's livid. 'That's not
what you were hired to do, you dumb broad! You
work for me!' " She wasn't laughing any more. "I
think 'dumb broad' is what did it. Till he said that, I
was almost ready to stay home like a nice little girl
with all those files. Know what, Tom? I think Maynard's jealous."

"And why not? Ye be ramming about with a
handsome bugger like meself, smooth operator like
Joe—he's not so bad looking, either."

"Cream of the crop, both of you."

Tom patted her knee affably. "What a darling ye
be, to recognize top quality when ye see it."

Tom was running code two for no particular reason that she could see. Gretchen leaned back and
savored this exciting tingle of anticipation she was
feeling. "Joe on his way over there?"

"Left a few minutes ago in me bug. He and Marie
will enter the front way, across the pedestrian
bridge. We go in the back, the gate on the Salt River
side. The director knows what's up. We have a couple people pushing brooms in coveralls. And Janet
James in a docent's jumper."

"What about me? Everyone concerned can recognize me, except that Barbrie fellow."

"Did ye see the videotapes of Barbrie?"

She nodded. "I'll know him if I see him."

"Then," said Tom, "we're in business. Yourself

and I are a team. We keep Joe and Marie in sight, but at a distance. And we're not just looking for the principals. Joe's pretty sure the killer has an accomplice and quite possibly someone completely unknown to us. The person who lifted the rental car so craftily at the airport, and probably got the bomb ingredients."

"The pickpocket?"

"Aye, and possibly in this as deep as our chief suspect. Dangerous, therefore."

"But that could be anyone. A stranger. Or Henry Barbrie. He fits the bill."

"True." Tom flicked his siren to pass a sluggish and inattentive recreation vehicle. "There should not be many visitors on a warm afternoon like this. So we'll simplify our job by suspecting everybody at the zoo."

"Marvelous." Gretchen watched the passing buildings, the pedestrians, an occasional bicycle. "Tom? Tell me something. How thick are Joe and Marie really?"

Tom glanced at her. "Getting tired of Maynard?"

"No fair answering a question with a question."

Tom shrugged. "Meself was heartily sick of Maynard Rust a month after I met him. Can't imagine how ye managed to hang in there all these years."

"Only two years with Maynard. I asked about Joe and Marie."

"Marie lights up like Christmas every time she sees 'im."

"And Joe?"

"Can't quite bring himself to get past her past, if ye see me meaning."

Gretchen nodded. "That's his one big fault; never thinks a woman's good enough for him. I don't know what his standards must be except that they're impossible. He's an iceberg."

"Meself couldn't agree with ye less. Most of the girls he's dated—the little dating he's done—are from the department and I've met 'em. Wouldn't have them meself. He deserves better."

"Like a murder suspect."

"Ye must admit, it makes a colorful entry in the 'occupation' blank of your marriage license."

She snickered. "Did you ever meet his Louise?"

"No. We paired up a couple months after it happened. He was in a black cloud for years. 'What a drupe for a partner' I be thinking to meself then. I've since revised me estimate of him considerably, of course. Infatuated with her, he was."

"Wonder what it's like to have a man so totally devoted to you as that. You know, Tom, if I died today, Maynard would have a new girl in his sack tomorrow and a smile on his face and no break in the schedule. Maybe get a little further behind with his paperwork, is all."

Tom's voice was so calm and gentle she nearly missed the significance of what he said. "Well, lass, ye just pop your sidearm out there and make sure it's ready to go. 'Cause I know one Irish cop who'd shed tears a-plenty were ye to die today."

Joe locked the car door on his side and crossed around to Marie's side. She was already out and had locked her door. He arranged his flapping shirt tail, making certain it hid the gun in his belt. He felt tense. He always felt tense about these setups—so much could go wrong—but this time it was particularly bad. How could Marie stay so calm?

They strolled casually across the lot. There was Mel Carter right over there, in coveralls. Joe had handpicked his crew for this trap, with Mel as numero uno. Joe admired Mel's quick, clear head. On the other hand, Joe always felt a little uneasy bringing a girl around him. Not that Mel was predatory exactly; he had his harem and didn't seem to bird-dog other men's women too much. But his good looks almost always charmed whoever he felt like charming. Joe suddenly realized he didn't want Mel Carter's charm anywhere near Marie Kabrhan.

The normally suave cop had refrained from shaving this morning, the better to look less polished. He wandered about now almost lackadaisically, plucking up gum wrappers and defunct paper cups. His gun was probably in the litter bag. He had already positioned himself to see that part of the parking lot Joe could not see. Joe appreciated Mel's professionalism.

Now Joe and Marie were stepping out onto the broad pedestrian bridge between parking and the gate. They were exposed here. Vulnerable. He wanted to hurry across, but Marie stopped at the railing to watch the ducks below.

"How do they get the ducks to stay here, Joe?"

"Most of them, they don't." He stood not beside her but close behind. "A few of them, they clip the flight feathers on one wing. And feed them. You know, the ducks were here before the zoo. My father talks about coming over here to Papago Park to watch the ducks. This was a game-and-fish facility. Just this pond and a couple other ponds and a little stone administration shack. No zoo yet, of course."

"You grew up with the zoo. And now your children are." She turned and they continued on across.

Mrs. Melton, the lady with the blue streak in her gray hair, was sitting in the kiosk today. As he handed her a guest pass for Marie, she surveyed the girl up and down and smiled warmly. Apparently his date had passed muster. "Good afternoon, Mr. Rodriguez. Have a nice visit."

"We'll try. Thanks, Mrs. Melton." They passed through the turnstile and paused by a small flight cage. The mynah garbled one of its unintelligible phrases.

"What did he say, Joe?"

"Who knows?" He glanced toward the flamingos. Deserted. "The zoo has a couple mynahs. This one's allowed to talk to the folks. The previous owner of one of the others taught it a different vocabulary. It's over in a soundproof glass cage by the birds of paradise. If they ever figure out what this one's saying, he might end up in solitary too."

She wagged her head. "What can people see in putting blasphemous words in poor innocent birds' mouths?"

Behind them Mel Carter came rambling across the bridge, pausing to watch the ducks, picking up bits.

The thing Joe dreaded most, a school group, babbled by on its way to the tram. Joe didn't expect trouble by the front entrance here, but what if he were wrong? Thirty noisy little children chattered along in double file. He steered Marie quickly off to the left toward the flamingos. The happy child noises faded into the safety of distance.

Joe started up the hill past the ungulates and toward the big cats. Up ahead, Purley Petersen, his 280 pounds of bulk crammed into coveralls, was forking hay over the fence to the buffalo.

Joe stopped beside him and pointed off toward the mule deer in the far corner. "Marie, this is 'Burly' Purley Petersen. Purley, Marie Kabrhan. You look like a sausage in that jumpsuit."

"Biggest they had too." Purley shook his head and pointed to the white-tailed deer next door. "Man about twenty-five, five-eight, Southeast Asian; Vietnamese or Cambodian or something. Acted nervous by the hornbill cage, then walked on around the hill toward the cats. Seemed to be watching for someone. I haven't seen any of your featured faces." He shaped his hands and fingers in the air like antlers.

Joe nodded. "Thanks, Burl." As they strolled off around the hill, he heard the hay barrow creak behind him.

Vietnamese or Cambodian or something. Persis had a Nam connection. Through her pimp, so did Marie. And then there was that guy at Valley Cathedral. Joe should have looked for a white Datsun in the parking lot. It had never occurred to him.

Marie shot a glance over her shoulder. "Except that his suit's a little tight, he looks just like a zoo employee."

"We borrowed him from Robbery because he

knows the place better than I do. He has five kids by three marriages and he gives each one of them a birthday party at the zoo every year."

Marie's hand, once loose on his arm, now gripped him like an eagle's clasp. "I realize I'm safe with Jesus, and I know I'm well covered by policemen. But I'm scared spitless anyway. Isn't that foolish?"

"No, sensible. You're the cheese in a mousetrap, all right, and there's a good chance the cheese could get nipped. How many years have I been in this business and I'm scared too. That's good. The day you quit being scared, you start taking chances."

She forced a giggle. "Being scared, then, is God's warning to cover your backside."

Joe liked that giggle. "Except that when the action's over, you're still scared for an hour. Fear wears off slowly." They were coming up out of the curve of the hill, up among cages and enclosures again.

"Fear? Or adrenalin?"

He stopped short involuntarily, then walked slowly on, pretending interest in the Barbary sheep on the distant hill ahead. The wheelbarrow behind him stopped at the antelope enclosure. Purley had seen her too. Had Marie?

She gasped and buried her face in Joe's arm. "Oh my God, no!"

She had.

Persis Magen stood over at the far end of the tiger enclosure, almost on the lion side. She casually nibbled at a candy bar as she watched the tigers stretch and pace.

Joe angled left toward the leopard cage, keeping himself between Marie and the distant Persis. She must not see them until he was certain all his people knew where she was. He gave the visitors in the area a fast once-over. None suggested either danger or Purley's Southeast Asian. Where was Tom? Joe couldn't see Tom. The fluttering behind his breastbone was fast becoming nausea.

At the far end of the lion enclosure, almost beside the rhinos, Janet appeared in her docent jumper. She studied the lions a moment, scrawled some note across a clipboard, then scratched her head with her pencil.

"Is that one of your people too?"

"Worked the jail until we brought her into Homicide last February. Sharp lady."

"She said something by scratching her head?" Marie looked him in the eye. "Joe, tell me these things. I want to help you. I want to help get Cat's murderer and I want to help you personally. But I want to know what's happening too."

"Janet just signaled that Jules Robinson is right behind her, coming this way." Where was Tom? Joe felt like bolting, like scooping Marie up and running out the back gate away from this nightmare. What if his guess was wrong?

He noticed three things at once: (1) In the brief time his attentions were elsewhere, Persis had disappeared. (2) Some urban cowboy in a loud shirt was necking with his girlfriend over by the oleander hedge, his back to the world. All you could see was his huge, brilliant white cowboy hat tipped back. And (3) here came the elephant right into the middle of it.

Joe had forgotten the elephant. When he was talking to the director, why had he not canceled the elephant? Every afternoon just before the free animal show in the arena by the children's section, the trainer rode his elephant around the zoo, advertising the performance. Joe knew that. Why had he not remembered? Now he must adjust the plan to accommodate that stupid elephant.

"When things start popping, you drop down flat on the ground. Flat. Instantly. Understand?"

"But what about you?"

"You stay down and I'll be able to concentrate on doing my job without worrying about you."

"I see." Her voice dropped. "Joe, there's Henry Barbrie right over there by the snack stand."

"I see him."

"But why is he here? Unless. . . ? I don't . . ."

Henry paused at this end of the tiger enclosure, looking mildly confused. He seemed to be seeking someone, or perhaps expecting someone. Absently, he wandered off, out of sight.

Joe took Marie's hand in his own and strolled toward the jaguar cage. How did that slippery fish Persis disappear so quickly and completely? He could only pray that either Diane or Purley could see her. Where was Tom? Why couldn't the elephant walk faster? It lumbered and swayed in slow motion. Now it blocked his view of Janet.

"Joe!" Back by the leopard Purley yelled. Hay flew as he scrambled for his gun. The Asian—the same fellow for sure who sat in the lecture hall that afternoon—stood on the retaining wall by the tiger compound. He gripped a long-barreled pistol in both hands, in a widespread parody of the Weaver stance that he must have seen in some Stallone movie.

Joe dived, dragging Marie to the ground ahead of him, and came down roughly on top of her. The gun popped, like a Datsun backfiring—the long barrel was a silencer. Slugs clanged into the pipe rail beyond them.

Raging frustration boiled up in him. This accomplice wasn't the person he wanted to expose. With the trap sprung prematurely, the real killer would slip away. Or wait. . . ! Was this the culprit, the only culprit?

Purley's gun boomed. As Joe rolled to his feet the young man leaped off the retaining wall and started running, away from Purley and away from Joe. The kid was an athletic cuss, limber and quick. With the perp's head start, neither Joe nor Purley would get near him. Where was Tom?!

Joe was twenty feet along in his pusuit of the gunman before his brain got through to his feet that he must stop. His responsibility was Marie's safety. Someone else must pursue their assassin. He skidded to a halt as that amorous cowboy in the white hat came running along the rock wall outside the tiger moat. At the far end, the big male tiger flicked to his feet and watched intently, tail twitching. As the cowboy made a vaulting leap from the wall to the elephant's back, his hat flew off. Tom's red shock flamed bright in the sun. He disappeared beyond the elephant in the general direction of the gunman. Joe heard the silencer pop again.

He turned toward Marie but she was already on her feet beside him. Tears darkened the dirt on her scuffed cheek where he had pushed her down. "Get him, Joe!" The tears were fury, not fear.

Joe saw Gretchen coming at a dead run toward them. "Gretch! Keep Marie!" Joe gave Marie a hard shove in Gretchen's general direction and took off to help Tom.

Then the world froze silent, motionless.

The erstwhile Asian assassin lay on his face in the granite dust beside the walkway. Tom's ornate boot was planted on the boy's neck, the gun arm twisted behind at a grotesque angle. Tom already had one cuff snapped on, but now he had stopped cold along with everything else. He was staring not at the helpless would-be assassin beneath his boot, but at their killer.

KING KONG AND THE ANGELS

Between the tiger enclosure and the snack bar, his hands trembling in the fear of a world gone haywire, stood Jules Robinson. The gun he carried, a foreign automatic with a maw .44 calibre at least, shimmied and bobbed, dancing on the tips of his nerves. It was pointed at Tom Flaherty's heart.

Jules' idea of a disguise was black moustache and sunglasses. He looked ludicrous. And deadly.

Jules shouted at Joe, "I should've known it was a trap. I suspected as much, but I should have known."

"That's why you invited Henry Barbrie to meet you here? Asked him to join you near the tiger compound? Then you'd have an easy mark to pin it on. You might wrestle him to the ground and claim you saw him do it. Or maybe you'd just toss the gun at his feet on your way out and let the cops draw their own conclusions. After all, he already has a police record—feds, yet. Pretty smart."

"Smarter than you think. I know that woman in the zoo dress is one of your people. The one who kept looking at me and pretending not to. Tell her to come around here in front where I can see her better."

Joe looked at Janet briefly. She edged around, sidestepping in reluctant obedience. She was watching Joe. Beside him, the nervous elephant stood weaving from foot to foot. The trainer was watching Joe. They were all watching Joe. It was his setup and it had gone down very crooked. Now they were waiting for him to pick up the pieces. He saw Marie's and Gretchen's legs beyond the elephant, the rest of them hidden by the hulk.

Marie had drawn from him a commitment to Jesus Christ, something he would never have dreamed he'd ever do. He was supposed to dump all his cares on Jesus and in turn take on Jesus' cares. What would Jesus want with this mess?

Joe held a hand up toward the trainer. "Don't move. Just leave Mathilda standing right there, will you?"

Tom dropped the accomplice's arm, cuff and all, and spread his own hands wide. "Ye recall, ye panicked once before, lad, at the motel. And ye regretted it sorely, immediately thereafter. We'd best sit down and talk this out before ye do anything else regrettable, aye?"

"Don't sweet-talk like that. I know what you're trying to do. Bring Marie out here. I want to see Marie."

"No, lad, we're afraid you'll hurt her." Tom gave his boot a little twist. "Yourself on the deck there, just lie still. Like a stone. Don't get into more trouble than ye got already. Hear me?" Tom stepped aside and moved toward the shrubbery and the retaining wall, putting space between himself and Joe.

Jules' gun followed him. "I just want to talk to her. That's all."

"Sorry, lad."

"I'll shoot you, I swear. You'll go first."

Joe heard scuffling beyond the elephant. Marie's "Let me go talk to him" was being seriously muffled by something across her mouth. Gretchen's vise grip would no doubt have held King Kong.

"You'll notice, lad, we didn't shoot this helper of yours, despite that he fired his weapon first and I'm carrying me own sidearm. Ye see it here?" Tom twisted slightly and pointed vigorously to his pocket. "Department protocol regarding deadly force permits us to blow ye away should we so choose, but we choose to avoid hurting anybody— even threatening sorts with large-calibre weapons. Ye'll be wise to do the same."

Joe tucked his shirttail in, making his own weapon visible. "I have mine too, Jules, but I haven't used it. I promise you this, though; anything happens to Tommy there, anything at all, you're dead in little pieces. I guarantee it."

Jules eyed the gun butt sticking out of Joe's belt for but a moment. "I don't care anymore. I'll make sure I . . . I want to talk to Marie. Bring her out here."

"You don't want to die before you get Persis. She's still running around loose, you know; still spreading her poison." Joe sidled toward the elephant, fragmenting and spreading the things Jules had to concentrate upon.

Jules' face melted, softened, assumed an almost hopeful look. "You saw through her lies too. She says God changes people. He doesn't. He didn't change me. He didn't take away any bad thoughts. I tried. I gave Him every chance in the world and He didn't change anything. He doesn't love me. He doesn't even exist. She's a liar."

"That car bomb. You're out to get Persis, Marie, and Cat, all three. Maybe even Henry too, or stick him with the rap. It didn't matter who or how many blew up. Why no more bombs after the one through the window? Run out of makings?"

"He wouldn't get me any more. Said he couldn't get me any more, so I have to use the gun."

"He. Your friend on the ground there?"

The Asian started to protest innocence. Tom hissed at him to shut up. Tom was over against the bushes now. With Jules already strung so tight, Joe was afraid Tom might be moving around too much.

Joe now stood beside Mathilda's massive shoulder. The elephant leaned toward him. His kids had ridden her and fed her a thousand peanuts. She knew him.

Purley and Janet, like Joe, were stymied. Where was Mel? Joe saw a light brown head bob beyond Jules, away down near the rhino compound.

"How did you get this fellow to go along with you, Jules, and help you out?"

Jules licked his lips. The moustache was skewing loose.

"Come on, Jules. The business is close enough done. Soon as you find Persis it'll be over."

"Not until I get . . . until I talk to Marie. And Persis. I'm doing the world a favor, believe me."

"Your helper there. How'd you find him?"

"Tulsa, the meetings . . . "

"How much do you pay him?"

"Don't have to. He understands. We're in it together. We're doing the world a favor."

"By ridding it of Persis Magen?"

"Of course. Call Marie out here. I want to see her."

"Why Marie and Cat, if your beef's with Persis?"

"Nits make lice. Besides, they're all just as bad. There's Brother Smith and Mr. Blake back in Waukesha too. They're spreading the lies. Hurting people. They're all liars."

"And greedy. Don't forget greedy. Cat wouldn't let you have any part of her payoff. Said she needed it all herself. That's greedy." Joe felt a certain pity, in spite of himself, for this twisted mind that couldn't perceive reality.

"Yes, yes!" Jules relaxed a bit more. The gun barrel didn't waver any more. "You see it too! Some sob story about a crippled boy, as if I would believe that. Liars. And they say they're so full of love too, but they aren't. No love in them at all."

"Turned you down, huh?"

"Worse. They laughed at me. The secretary across the hall, the legal secretary. She was blond. Just perfect. They poisoned her mind about me. 'Water cooler romance.' They refused me and they turned her against me."

"Ever ask Persis to marry you?"

"Of course. It was the honorable thing. I would have provided well for her too. I have resources. When she said no, that's when I started thinking God doesn't change you. I prayed Him to change her—change her mind—and He didn't."

"So when you met this fellow in Tulsa you set him straight."

"He said he wanted to believe her, but I showed him the truth. He realizes Persis is spreading lies. God didn't change him either. We talk about it all the time, him and me. Lies."

"He's the pickpocket who stole the car for you at Sky Harbor."

Jules turned tense and purple instantly. "He squealed! He told you! I hate squealers!"

"Nonsense," Tom cooed. "We don't need squealers. We learn everything by investigating. Everything. Take your name, for instance. We know 'tis Richard Lee Spesch. We've known that all along."

"That's impossible! You can't possibly know that. My records are all sealed by court order." His voice dropped a bit. "You can't . . . " Confusion was starting to outweigh determination in Jules' addled face. A few more little blockbusters and they just might talk him into letting Tom make his decisions for him. Except they didn't have any more blockbusters.

Mel was working his way in behind Jules, less than fifty feet away now. He crouched just beyond a litter receptacle shaped like a huge pink kangaroo, then moved forward again.

Tom stood near the 4 by 8 foot display explaining the world distribution of rhinoceroses. Joe noticed movement beyond the display board.

Persis stepped out into the open. She was too far away. Tom could never reach her, not in time.

No wonder she was such a brilliant orator. Even when she spoke in low, dulcet tones without aid of an amplifier, she echoed. "Here I am, Jules. Face me."

Jules wheeled, transfixed. The gun wavered, from Tom to Persis to Tom.

Persis stepped forward a few feet. "We discussed angels once, Jules. Do you remember our conversation about guardian angels? You believe God is false. Very well. Then angels must be, also. If angels don't exist, surely you can kill me now, without interference. Here I am."

That insane woman! Joe searched desperately for some way to get her out from under Jules' sites. Nothing. He was too far away to jump Jules; Tom was too far away to pull Persis down.

So much for professionalism. Mel bumped into that litter receptacle. The hollow fiberglass clunk broke the stalemate.

With a shriek to scare banshees, Jules wheeled and blasted wildly at the pink kangaroo. Tom lunged toward Persis as Joe dived for Jules. Behind him he heard the elephant trumpet; huge padded feet shook the ground in the haste of departure.

Tom and Persis disappeared in a tangle in the shrubbery. Jules swung toward them and fired. Joe would be too late . . .

He slammed into Jules. His legs kept pumping, dragging the gangling assailant down in a windmill of arms and legs. A sharp elbow rammed the pit of Joe's stomach; henceforth he'd have to operate without breathing. Jules wrenched free. That infernal gun blasted again.

As Joe lurched to his knees, he saw a flurry of flowered skirts beyond Jules, heard Gretchen screaming aspersions on Jules' cleanliness and ancestry. Gretchen hit Jules just as Joe managed to haul erect on his one good leg. Gretch and Joe splacked together like cymbals, with Jules in the middle. Joe's knees buckled, but that was all right — all the easier to mash Jules' gun arm into the dirt. The gun roared once more. Resistance melted as Jules' arm went limp. Joe ripped the gun away and groped for his cuffs.

Gretchen was gasping and gulping air, her hand on her solar plexus, but she kept one beautiful knee firmly planted on Jules' neck. Her eyes met Joe's and she grinned brightly, victoriously. Joe handed her his cuffs. With triumphant flourish, she put Jules under lock and key.

Joe could see Jules' face now. The fake moustache, loosened by sweat, had slipped completely. It hung by one-half to his cheek. Ludicrous.

Mel and Janet and the Burl arrived. Purley yanked the Asian accomplice to his feet in one powerful handful. None of Burl's seventh of a ton was fat. Joe struggled to standing.

Tom. The checkered shirt hovered above the shrubbery by the display board. Marie was there too. Tom and Marie pulled in unison; Persis came popping out of a dense little creosote bush. She rocked slightly and reassumed her air of regal authority. What did it matter that she was sprinkled liberally with dry and crackly little creosote leaves?

Gretchen could barely speak. "Why didn't you blow him apart while his back was turned?"

"I had every intention—I don't know why I didn't." Joe had not realized until that moment that his own gun was still tucked away in his belt. "Wonder how they're doing with their elephant stampede. Mathilda should be back home by now." Joe's hands shook worse than Jules' had. Maybe Marie was right. Maybe this was adrenaline rather than fear.

Persis came over to stand by his side. He had never seen eyes as sad as hers as they rested on Jules. "I see everyone is all right. I put all of us under the cover of prayer before I showed myself. Prayer for safety. That Satan be bound. Obviously, the safety included Jules. I'm glad."

Joe laughed suddenly. The weight of the world wafted away. "Queen Kong here, and the guardian angels. Right." He sobered. "Persis, you thought all along it was him, didn't you?"

"I wasn't sure."

"Why didn't you at least voice your suspicions to us?"

"By what authority? When Brother Larry Jennings launched his phone campaign, I perceived that I myself was a strong suspect. And I had no evidence, not even circumstantial evidence. I could see him drifting away from the Word, but how would that sound to the police ear? Tell me. How did *you* know?"

"Yeah! How did you peg him?" Gretchen stepped back as a black and white pulled up beside them. Lanky Harry Wallace unfolded from the driver's seat, a giraffe among tigers, to take over Jules' custody.

"There's nothing in Henry Barbrie's records to suggest pickpocketing. More important, Henry has trouble with gross coordination. A dip has to have excellent coordination; a soft, sure, gentle touch. And yet Jules very carefully fingered Barbrie as a pickpocket. Why? Unless he knew that we were looking for one. And that means he would know why. So he implicated Henry."

"There be one possible glitch—and a biggie." Tom chimed in. "That would be if yourself, Marie, had tipped off Jules to the pickpocket business without realizing it. In idle chitchat, for example. For we talked about how the car was stolen at the airport as ye sat between us, remember?"

"I never mentioned . . . "

"We were both pretty sure ye would not, for ye seemed not to be in a close rapport with your compatriot here."

"That was the big unknown in this." Joe nodded. "But we were both fairly confident it didn't leak there, enough that we took this flyer."

Gretchen's head was bobbing knowingly up and down. "Everything fits. He finds his partner in Tulsa, the partner supplies him with his plastiques, he uses the leather bag to keep it in. He has lots of free time in Phoenix, since he's not in Riverside, to set it up with his pal. The bombs don't work so he switches to guns. Then Marie gets herself tucked away safely in the clink, Persis is surrounded by cops and he's fresh out of targets, until he hears about Marie's date here. The threatening notes were simply to get Persis worried. You don't want to bump off somebody before they know what's coming. You want them to stew awhile."

Tom grinned. "Gretchen, lass, ye should be a detective."

"I thought I was."

Harry's hand was on Jules' neck to thrust him down into the car, but Jules snapped upright suddenly. "You, Marie. You and Cat. You gave your loves to all the men in the world. Hundreds of men. But you wouldn't give any loves to me."

Marie stood so close to Joe he could feel her warmth and presence on his arm. "Before, Jules. Cat and I were that way *before* we met the Lord. We changed."

"And Jules," Persis called, "Cat really does have a son, and Eric really is a spina bifida victim. She couldn't afford to pay you off. She had none to spare."

Harry's hand prevailed. Jules disappeared into the back seat. Harry hopped in and drove over to Purley.

"Mrs. Magen, why didn't you mention Jules' marriage proposal?"

"The classic reply, Mr. Rodriguez—you never asked. I had honestly forgotten all about it. It was over a year ago. You see, when you bring someone to the Lord, that person sometimes develops a special affection for you. I receive several marriage proposals a month. I was in error to count Jules' intentions so lightly; I see that now."

Joe sighed. His ribs hurt. At least his hands weren't shaking any more. "That leaves the ticket. Tommy? Where's Rocinante?"

"Coming." Tom pointed past the rhinos. The tired old prowl car wheezed to a halt before them.

Janet climbed out. "Up to driving, Tommy?"

"Aye, thanks."

Janet nodded and walked off toward Harry and Burl and their perpetrators.

Joe had guessed right.

Tom waved a hand toward Rocinante. "Persis? Gretch?"

Marie sputtered, instantly defensive. "Where are you taking her?"

"To the airport, lass. She has exactly ninety-seven minutes to flight time. Surely ye didn't forget she must be in Riverside tonight." He held the far door open. Gretchen slipped in, with Persis right behind. "Ye might tell me, Mrs. Magen, why ye came to the zoo this afternoon."

"When Miss Wiemer stopped by to mention that Marie would be released, I smelled something like this—an attempt to nab the culprit. I wanted to be here to help, if possible. But my primary motivation was pure curiosity—a burning desire to—"

Rocinante's door slammed, cutting off the sound of her voice. It slammed twice more. Tom hopped behind the wheel and the blue lights came to life a lot more enthusiastically than did the engine. Maybe Joe could tune it a little better some afternoon.

With the whole zoo to stand in, Marie was parked

so close to Joe he could feel her body move as she breathed.

Mel Carter wagged his head. "Sorry about bumping the can. I didn't think I was that close to it. Hey, you should see what a .44 Magnum does to a fiberglass kangaroo."

"No apologies needed. You know what Henry Barbrie looks like. He's still wandering around the grounds somewhere. Think you can find him?"

"Sure. Treat him to a zebra cola and take him back to his motel. Might even pick up some gum wrappers along the way." Mel graced Marie with a dazzling smile and ambled off.

Joe rejoiced to see Lothario leave.

Marie was looking up at Joe. She said nothing, but those big gorgeous eyes were speaking. *What about me? What about us?* Joe had thought that out last night too. Tommy was right. Tommy was almost always right about such things. He knew people.

Joe would explain to her that now he understood better about clean slates. It would be tough; it would really be tough, to shove himself past his own moral objections. But then, he was the only one who clung to them. Everyone else accepted her for what she appeared to be—a woman worth hanging onto at any cost. If the kids and Tommy did, he would.

And God. Joe had spent his whole life avoiding religious fanaticism, especially the Jesus freaks. Now here he was spouting their line—depending for eternity upon a Jesus he was only just beginning to know. Joe liked hard evidence in black and white. The way this bust had just gone down was strong evidence that God really does intervene where you need Him. They should all have Jules' bullets in them right now, Persis especially.

How did Marie put it? Something like, "Forget me, forget the Jesus people, forget what anyone else thinks. This must be between you and God, one on one." Marie knew about such things, just as Tommy knew about people.

He would ask her forgiveness for his previous attitude, his prior ignorance. But that would come later, at a better time than this.

He didn't feel like walking the road around. He draped his arm across her shoulders and started off cross-country, directly over the hill toward the front gate and Tom's green bug. Their feet scritched in the pink gravel.

She sobbed a single, shuddering sigh. "I feel so sorry for Jules."

"Bet Persis is back here in Phoenix the first chance she gets, trying to bring him back into the fold."

"And that other young man. Persis has a very special spot in her heart for Vietnamese. For all Southeast Asians." She matched strides with him as if she'd grown up at his side. "Joe? Can I get to Riverside some way, to help Persis? She really needs me now."

"We have a lot of paperwork to do on you yet, but I think so. Late night flight, probably."

She nodded. Silence. "Nice zoo. I like your zoo."

He enjoyed her closeness immensely. In fact, he was astonished at how good he felt with her pressed against him. "We have Ruby, the artistic elephant who creates paintings. And our oryx-breeding program is the best. And the zoo's growing. New stuff, renovation, new displays. It's big."

"Mm hmm." More silence. "Joe? Do we really have to go look at those stupid orangutans?"